BOOK 4
THE PEAKS SAGA

WHEN the WORLD GROWS COLD

M.F. ERLER

WHEN THE WORLD GROWS COLD, Book 4
by M.F. Erler

Published by

WESTWIND PRESS
an imprint of First Steps Publishing
PO Box 571
Gleneden Beach, Oregon 97388-0571
FirstStepsPublishing.com

ISBN: 978-1-937333-86-7 (hb)
           978-1-937333-82-9 (pb)
           978-1-937333-87-4 (epub)

Bible quotes are from New International Version:
"Scripture taken from Holy Bible, New International Version (Registered Trademark) Copyright
1973,1978, 1984 by International Bible Society. Used by permission of Zondervan Publishing
House. All rights reserved."

Lyrics to songs by Gregory A. DeMuth,
    Copyright 2005: Sacred Ground Music, used by Permission
All other lyrics quoted are Public Domain, or composed by the author.

Cover illustration by Kabita Studios
Cover design, interior formatting by Suzanne Fyhrie Parrott

Please provide feedback

10 9 8 7 6 5 4 3 2

Printed in U.S.A.

Praise for the Peaks Saga...

"I remember fondly reading The Lion, The Witch, and The Wardrobe *when I was in middle school.* The Peaks at the Edge of the World *has a similar mix of fantasy and adventure with a moral tale at its center. This is a book that's appropriate for a younger audience than most sci fi/fantasy novels. Enjoy the read!"*

—Kathy Dunnehoff
ZOLA AWARD-WINNING WOMEN'S FICTION WRITER

"...a page turner!" —Judith Seidel

"Ms. Erler puts religion in new settings as she uses the characters in both the past and the future to meld the consequences of a religion lost, then found, then challenged. The ride is exciting. The characters real and engaging."

—Charlene Hecht
BA MUSIC EDUCATION
LONGTIME WRITER, INCLUDING "GUNSMOKE" FAN FICTION

"M.F. Erler skillfully pioneers a new writing genre, mixing elements of science fiction, dimensional time-travel, and modern Christian spirituality. She uses likeable characters in well-crafted settings in which we can identify with their real-life struggles."

—Richard Bartlett, MA, PhD

"...[M.F.] Erler's book, with its futuristic sci-fi focus and true-to-life grittiness, is not your typical Christian novel. At times, it unabashedly describes the realities of the darkness of humanity in order to contrast it with the power of hope and love found in God's grace. This unique book is well worth your time to read and I highly recommend it."

—Pastor Kevin Bueltmann
TRINITY LUTHERAN CHURCH - ASSOCIATE PASTOR
TRINITY LUTHERAN CAMP - EXECUTIVE DIRECTOR

Books by M.F. Erler

THE PEAKS SAGA

PEAKS AT THE EDGE OF THE WORLD
Finding the Light

SEARCHING FOR MAIA

MOUNTAINTOPS AND VALLEYS

WHEN THE WORLD GROWS COLD

THE FOUNTAIN AND THE DESERT

BEYOND THE WORLD

WHERE ALL WORLDS END

This book is dedicated to
All those who are out there searching,
—as I was—and sometimes still am.

Contents

"They went about in sheepskins and goatskins, destitute, persecuted and mistreated—the world was not worthy of them. They wandered in deserts and mountains, and in caves and holes in the ground."

— Hebrews 11:37-38

ACKNOWLEDGMENTS

Kurt, who because of his firm faith and honesty has helped me look at many things in a different way. I appreciate it a lot, Kurt, even though I haven't followed your advice in everything!

Pastor Greg, whose heartfelt music has been there for me on many a dark day. Wish that I could have put the music in along with the lyrics.

Char, who has always been there for me, with honest criticism, as well as encouragement—the kind of friend you can be totally honest with, and they put up with you anyway.

Suzanne, who is so much more than a business associate and publisher. I'm looking forward to the day we meet face-to-face.

FOREWORD

Many people have walked by the hunk of rock called Christianity, lying half-buried in the sands of time. Most glance at the exposed part of this boulder and assume they know what the whole thing looks like—for good or ill.

But the author's task in fiction, especially fantasy, is to ask, "What if…" and then create a possible scenario—a fiction which may or may not come to pass in some distant future. (Some things predicted in science fiction have come to pass, though many have not—yet.)

Being the "rock hound" that my father was, I stop at this boulder and chip away at it with my geologist's hammer, exposing the new and unweathered shapes and colors inside—that few realized were there. (By the way, even so-called 'ordinary' rocks look amazing when they're put in water.)

If I'm strong enough, I turn the whole boulder over to examine the underside of it, and see what dwells beneath it. And what do I find? More "What ifs…!"

This book is not meant to be an exposition of Biblical prophecy—or a defense of any particular doctrine or philosophy. Instead, it is merely a journey of my imagination, a possible scenario of what the future might hold. And perhaps, as readers take this journey with me, they will discover a few answers to their questions--and probably some "What ifs" of their own.

The Sullien Family Tree

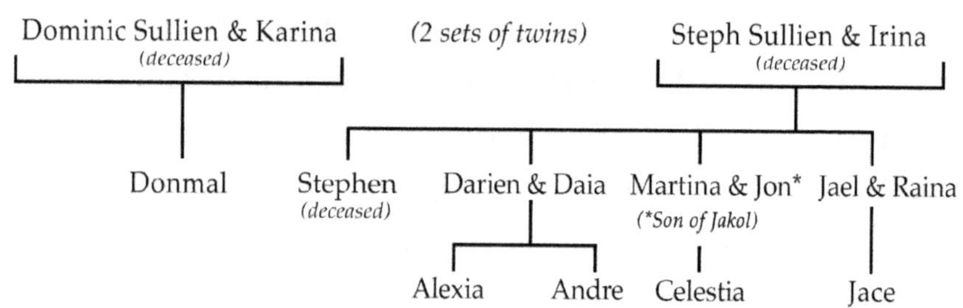

Dominic Sullien & Karina
(deceased)

(2 sets of twins)

Steph Sullien & Irina
(deceased)

Donmal

Stephen
(deceased)

Darien & Daia

Martina & Jon*
*(*Son of Jakol)*

Jael & Raina

Alexia   Andre   Celestia   Jace

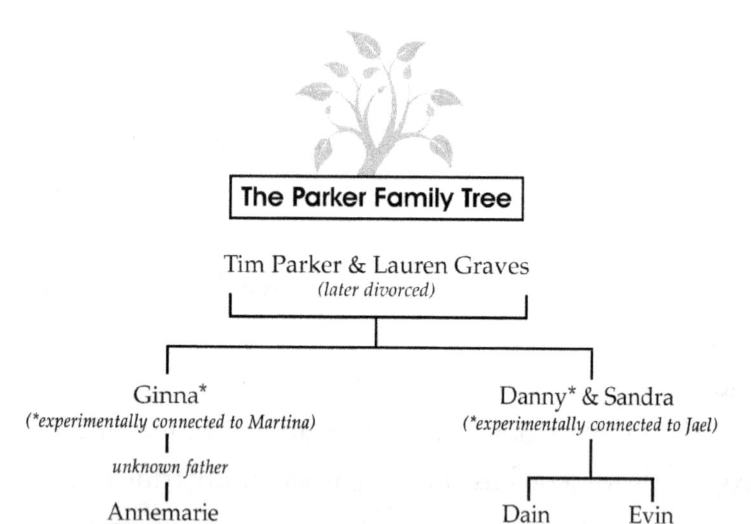

The Parker Family Tree

Tim Parker & Lauren Graves
(later divorced)

Ginna*
*(*experimentally connected to Martina)*

Danny* & Sandra
*(*experimentally connected to Jael)*

unknown father

Annemarie

Dain   Evin

CHAPTER 1

PRELUDE
AMID THE SNOW

Annemarie Parker leaned out the open hotel window, watching a world of softly drifting flakes, while the wind teased her long blonde hair. For an instant, she could visualize herself out there, floating slowly with those flakes, drifting ever downward, coming at last to rest in a wet spot on the sidewalk below.

'Just to rest. That's what I need,' she thought.

But her only movement was to hold out her hand and watch as the white fluffy flakes landed there, began to sag and settle, and finally disappeared, in tiny wet drops that slipped through her fingers. Just like her thoughts—sagging, melting, and disappearing into a dark chill night.

Her eyes tried to focus through the swirling whiteness. Out there loomed the indistinct shapes of downtown Denver, buildings that should be looking back at her with lighted windows for eyes, but this night they were blurred shapes, with their lights diffused by the snow in the air. Now her eyes began to blur, but not from the snow. These drops were warm, and fell onto her cheeks.

'There are too many memories here,' she sighed to herself. 'I should never have come back.'

Her ears could almost hear the strumming of guitars—hers and David's—and the singing of their Gospel group, along with the laughter of friends long-gone from her life. 'Yes, we used to sing here a lot, in this very hotel—there was a youth gathering right after Christmas every year.'

The words of the songs had meant so much then: 'The Old Rugged Cross' and 'Love Lifted Me'.

And there was always lots of snow, which made it all the more cozy. The memories seemed to shine like Christmas, as she saw them now in her mind. So many times she'd sat at a window, just like this, watching the snow turn the world into a dream—a place of beauty and love.

But she'd been much younger then—what was it? Nearly eight years ago? Life hadn't seemed so confusing at that time—everything had been more simple and natural, like the first time David held her hand.

He'd been walking her home from church—back in their little hometown of Deer Path, Colorado. They sang almost every Sunday when they were in high school. Gradually other members of their Gospel group moved on to college or jobs, until she and David were the only ones left.

Her mother, Ginna Parker, usually drove home before Annemarie was ready to leave. Mom didn't stay to visit much after church. Most of the time, David had a new song he wanted her to learn, and they'd practice for almost an hour before heading home. But Deer Path was so small, anyone could walk from one end to the other in an hour or less.

Sometimes Uncle Danny hung around to listen to them practice. He seemed to really enjoy their music. Annemarie knew her mother could take it or leave it. But Ginna's life hadn't been easy, she knew. After all, when a local girl got pregnant and decided to keep the baby, that was big news in such a small town. Besides, Ginna and her brother Danny were always considered outsiders, not having spent their whole lives in Deer Path. Annemarie had—at least through high school.

But she seemed to have a restless nature. She never met her father, or even knew his name. No one seemed to be able to tell her anything about him. Ginna refused to say anything—ever—about this mystery man. So Annemarie lived with the whispers. Was he a drifter who was just passing through? Perhaps someone else in the town? Only Ginna knew, and she'd apparently worn herself to silence.

Growing up with all the talk behind her back—and even to her face—Annemarie knew she must be very careful. Her mother seemed to sigh with relief when she began spending time with David. He was the pastor's son, and apparently wanted to live up to his father's expectations. It wasn't surprising, then, that they walked across the small town many Sundays before he finally took her hand.

Now she tried to remember the thrill of that first touch. It had been such a strong feeling then—a warmth coursing all through her body. Their hands seemed to fit together perfectly, as though they were made for each other. And later, there was the first kiss.

But all these memories were getting blurred now—as hazy and fuzzy as the snow-filled world outside her window. A large tear plopped on the windowsill, and her heart ached with the questions she couldn't answer.

'What happened? Which of us changed? How could something seeming so right go so wrong? Perhaps I've inherited a curse from my mother,' she said to herself. She didn't want to blame Ginna, but sometimes she couldn't help it. 'Her choices—bad or not—have caused me a lot of pain,' she muttered. But then she sighed, for she knew if she was honest, most of her pain was caused by her own choices—and there was really no one else to blame but herself.

She stood and shivered, reaching toward the top of the window. Just as she was trying to get up the courage to climb onto the sill, she saw a shape out there in the snow-filled air. It seemed to be a face, but the eyes were like stars shining, and the long hair was billowing out into the cold air, like sails on a great ship. She gasped in fear and froze, unable to close the window or to drop her hand from the sash.

Then a gust of wind rushed past her face. She could see swirls of white as snow whirled into the room. Stepping back, she covered her face with her hands, trying not to scream. When she slowly pulled her hands down and tried to focus her eyes, there was a young woman with long dark hair standing in the room with her.

A long-ago conversation with her mother came into her mind, and she remembered a name: "Martina?" she said. "Mom mentioned someone with that name once, but I don't remember anything else, except that she had long, dark hair—and she took her somewhere."

"Well, I'm her daughter, Celestia. Did she tell you anything about me?"

Annemarie glanced down at the floor and tried to think, but her mind was just a whirl. A few minutes ago, she'd been contemplating suicide, and now here she was talking to this stranger who appeared out of the sky. 'Am I hallucinating?' she wondered.

Finally, she found her voice, "No, I don't remember anything else. Mom was always very close-mouthed about her past. She never told me anything about my father."

"Okay," Celestia sighed. "Well, to start with, I'm a GAP-Crosser—or what some might call a time-traveler. Jon, my father, is the one who's done the most exploration of the Time-GAP's possibilities, and he taught me some of what he knows. At first, GAP-crossing was used mainly to travel great distances through the Galaxy. Only first-born have the power to learn to manipulate the GAP, which stands for Galactic Antipaterminal Passage, by the way. This dimension of space/time has always existed, but here in your time people haven't yet discovered this potential of the first-born. I guess right now, you might call it a sort of 'worm hole'."

"I've heard that term in science classes," Annemarie nodded. "But what does all this have to do with me? And how did you get here?"

"I crossed the GAP," she smiled. "My father and my Uncle Jael have learned how to cross Time-GAPs."

"You mean like a Time Portal?"

"Yeah, I think that's what they called it back in this century."

"So, you're from the future?" It was difficult to keep the disbelief out of her voice.

Celestia just smiled and nodded to her. "I can't explain all the technical stuff. All I know is what Dad taught me. About twenty-five years ago, in Earth years, he and Jael came to your mother and your Uncle Danny."

"Here to Colorado?"

"Yes, to their little town of Deer Path."

"That's where I grew up—and I'm twenty-five years old now."

"I know." Again, Celestia smiled, and this time there seemed to be some secret knowledge in her expression. "Anyway, they took your mom, Ginna, and her brother to their time—into the distant future, to share their stories with them. Actually, they crossed the GAP more than once. The last time, Dad did an experiment that had something to do with parallel universes."

"Now wait a minute—this is starting to sound like science fiction." Annemarie shook her head in disbelief. "Are you just making this up as you go along?"

Celestia patted her arm. "No, I'm trying to tell you the truth. It appears you've called me, like your mother did mine."

In her conscious mind, Annemarie wanted to pull away from Celestia's touch, but something in her subconscious held her back. The longer she felt that gentle touch, the calmer she began to feel. "Okay," she sighed, "I'll suspend my disbelief—for now."

"I'm glad, because this gets even stranger." Again, Celestia had a knowing smile in her eyes. "What Jon, my father, did was merge Danny with Jael, and Ginna with Martina, my mother. They became like two minds in one body."

"They what? Okay, I'm really having trouble with this."

"I know, Annemarie." Again, the woman's touch seemed to be saying even more than her voice. "It's really difficult to explain. But while your mother was 'within' *my* mother, Martina, she experienced everything with her. They were both 'there', in a sense. Did your mom ever tell you anything about this?"

Annemarie shook her head, but then stopped as an image came into her mind. "All she ever said was the name Martina once, and a strange journey they'd taken together. But there was one other time, when I was about fourteen years old. We were sitting on a new living-room couch we'd just bought. Suddenly her eyes seemed to get a far-away look in them and I heard her whisper, 'I wonder if it was something in the old couch that made it possible.' I asked her what she meant, but she suddenly shook her head, and seemed not to remember even saying anything. Then she looked out the window and added, 'I think it was all a dream'."

"Dad has said many people think of it as a dream. But I'm here to prove to you, and maybe your mother, that it really did happen."

"So, what happens now? Do you take *me* to some other place or time?"

"Actually, this time is different. First you get to tell me your story."

"You don't really want to hear my story," she muttered. "It's not a pretty one."

"Well, the ones my parents came to share with your mother and uncle weren't exactly pretty, either. But they were true, and they taught them some truths about life, and the Lord of the Universe."

"You mean God?"

"Yes, some people call him that."

"So, you think my story can teach *you* something?"

Celestia shrugged. "Perhaps. And someday, I may be able to share mine with you. I think we can both learn something from each other. But my directions said you were to start first."

"Your directions? Who gave those?"

"I can't explain in a way you'll understand right now. Maybe later."

"Okay. So, this means I have to start, I guess."

"In a minute. First I need to get this lamp lit."

Celestia produced an amber-colored lamp with a strange fluted chimney—Annemarie had no idea where it came from. She set it on the bedside table, because there wasn't another level spot in the small hotel room. Annemarie didn't see how she lit it, but soon swirls of gold, amber, and brown were slowly moving around the walls of the room.

The two young women sat down on the bed at the same time. This brought shy smiles to both their faces. Then Celestia reached over and took Annemarie's hands in hers, and again there seemed to be a warm calm flowing into her from the time-traveler's touch.

"You may start anytime you feel ready," she said. "I'm

firstborn and can cross the GAP. And the Lantern will take us wherever we may need to go, especially in the fourth dimension—Time."

CHAPTER 2

ANNEMARIE'S TALE

I was truly in love with David, the best I knew how to love at age seventeen. So, I can't really put a finger on when things changed. It was all so subtle and gradual. In my mind it's all gray and hazy, like that sky out there full of snow, or like a smoke-filled room—and I've seen too many of them, I'm afraid.

As soon as he graduated from high school, David prepared to go to the Bible college over on the West Slope—that's what we Coloradoans call the other side of the Continental Divide. He gave me a promise ring, and then drove away to study to be a minister, like his father.

"Why can't I come with you?" I pleaded.

"I just don't feel we're ready to be married so young," he said.

"But I love you! What makes you an expert on marriage, anyway?"

"You're barely out of high school."

"Same as you."

He took me in his arms and kissed me. "Just as soon as I can get settled over there, I promise I'll come for you. I just don't want to drag you into the unknown. I feel it's my responsibility to prepare things for us. We're not even ready to say we're engaged yet."

"But I could help you. Please let me come with you and be a part of this." In my mind, I wished this ring was a true engagement ring, but he insisted it wasn't 'time yet.'

'Maybe he's not sure he really loves me,' I thought. 'Maybe his male ego is in the way.' And so, a seed of doubt was planted.

[Celestia chuckled at this. "You'll have to ask my mother about male egos."

"I hope I get to someday."]

Anyway, he'd gone off to Bible college, but Mom didn't have enough money to send me to college, and my grades weren't good enough for any scholarships. I hoped that I could work and earn enough to begin taking some classes at a community college someday. And I needed something to fill my time, so I worked a part-time job at a café on the edge of town. Then I heard they had an opening at their nearby motel in Denver, and I asked to be transferred there. It seemed like a good time to leave Deer Path and all its troubles behind.

Not long after I'd started working at the *Denver Matador*, I saw an ad for music at their bar, so I applied. I loved to play and sing with my guitar. And despite my young age, only eighteen, they said I could play there until midnight.

It wasn't long before I had a small following of friends and acquaintances from Denver, and even little nearby towns like Deer Path. I think some of the Deer Path people just came to see the strange girl who had 'no father'. But after a little while, they seemed to keep coming back, so they must have liked my music. I was really excited when the bar owner actually put my name on his outdoor sign: "Music by Annemarie."

I poured myself into the music, striving to become the song itself, to really feel and communicate the emotions behind the words. The lights and smoke began to seep into me, and I found myself feeling very comfortable there on the tiny stage. Mellow, as we often called it back then.

One night I saw the bartender, Ed, watching me intently as I sang. I hadn't really noticed him much before. His eyes seemed to be trying to capture me almost, and I found myself singing to those gray eyes.

As nights went by, I looked into his eyes more and more. He wasn't what you'd call handsome—stocky and blond, and in about his mid-twenties. But there was something attracting me in his smile and the way his eyes sparkled.

The next weekend, when my break came, he set a beer

on the bar in front of him and nodded to me. I knew 3.2% beer was legal for eighteen-year-olds in Colorado, so I wandered over and sat down on the barstool.

"Hi, Annie," he said. "Have one on me." Then he winked and whispered, "It's not the unleaded stuff, either."

I took a sip. It was the real stuff, alright, full 6% beer. But no one would question him serving me a beer. They didn't know what percent it was.

Usually, I disliked being called 'Annie.' It had been Mom's pet name for me when I was little, and I didn't enjoy being reminded of my childhood. But with him it didn't seem to matter.

"I really like your singing," he said. "Do you write any of your own stuff?"

"A little bit." I still felt shy with him. There was something about his eyes that seemed to see right into my soul. There was a new sort of connection here I'd never felt before.

"You should sing some of it," he said. "People like to hear new songs, too."

"Oh, I don't know."

"Do one for me, then," he smiled.

"Well, maybe."

A couple of nights later, I set a piece of handwritten music on the stand in front of me. "This one's for Ed, the world's best bartender," I said. I saw him stop for a few seconds and look at me, as I began to sing my new song:

"When first I met you, I knew your face,
Somehow, I felt I'd known you before—
But not from words others had said.
Now I know you really care—
We have common hopes and dreams,
There before we even met;
All we need to do now is share."

I felt self-conscious, knowing my poetry was awkward. But when I finished, his eyes were still gazing into mine. Soon, it seemed every song I sang was for him.

After this, my breaks were always at the bar if he was on duty. It seemed some new life was flowing in my veins, as I sat there sipping beer and talking to Ed. Sensations swept me along on some strange wave, like the way the beer carried my mind along. After a break, I always felt somehow more in tune with the message of the music, but I wasn't sure if it was him or just the drinks.

When David came back at the end of the fall term, he was full of new ideas and doctrines he'd been learning. He even came to look me up in Denver, but he wasn't happy about my new job.

"You should quit that job right now," he said, as soon as I told him about it. "That's not something a future minister's wife should be doing."

I knew he had a point, but the tone of his voice, like he was scolding a child, really bugged me. "Oh, is this too much for you? Can't I make my own decisions? For your information, I love this job. I feel I have something important to share with people in my music."

"There are other places to share music than in a bar," he retorted.

"People there have needs, too. Maybe even more than people in church. Besides, who said I ever wanted to be a minister's wife anyway?"

I wasn't sure where this last line came from. But I found myself following it up with a dramatic toss of his promise ring, right onto the floor at his feet.

He called back later and tried to apologize. But I was still hurting, feeling my bruised pride. Then he asked, "Can we just start over? I'm sorry if I made you angry."

"Let's give it more time," I said, keeping my voice even and unemotional. "Like you said before, we're too young to get married now. I think we both need to do some growing up."

I felt some sort of elation at turning his own words back on him.

He went back to school, and I went back to my job.

***

After this, I found myself letting Ed give me a ride home sometimes. It meant I stayed much later, while he closed the place down. And I told myself I just liked the opportunity to talk with him more casually, away from the bar.

One night, he stopped his car just past a bridge, at a spot overlooking the South Platte River. Lights from downtown reflected off the black, still water. It made me think of a scene from some old black-and-white movie. Then I felt him slip his arm around me, drawing me closer to him. His kiss was so warm and deep that I felt like I was melting into his embrace.

"Let's go to my place," he whispered, caressing my neck with his lips.

My heart was pounding, and soon another black river seemed to be flowing deep inside of me. I couldn't say a word, but knew this would be a big mistake.

"I'm not ready for this," I finally managed to murmur.

"What? Are you that naïve?" he muttered. "Surely you're not a virgin!!"

"But I am," tears were beginning to burn my eyes now. "Please, just take me home."

I could feel the heat of his anger radiating toward me, as he pulled his arm away and re-started the car. "If you insist. But this is a mistake."

"I'm sorry, but I need to know if you love me."

He didn't reply.

I can't tell you what my feelings but I was in a whirling sea of colors fading in and out. I couldn't examine them too closely for fear of what I might find. He didn't say another word as he drove me home.

✳✳✳

The next Sunday, when the bar was closed, he had a party at his place. He invited people I knew vaguely from the bar, but no one from my Deer Path group of friends was there. The atmosphere was tense, especially when Ed looked over at me—his eyes piercing and questioning. I don't really remember much of the evening because I was drinking real liquor. Another bad idea. No one drew me into any of their conversations, so I just kept on drinking instead.

Ed seemed to be taking time to talk to everyone but me. All I could do was try to make conversation with a guy next to me named Mark, who I'd only just met. Everything was becoming a blur, brought on by vodka and tequila. I tried to get myself to wonder what was going on here.

Then suddenly, it seemed everyone was getting ready to leave. I was getting no signals from Ed. Did he want me to stay, or not? When I stood up, the room seemed to whirl, and I would've liked to lean on him. Dimly I felt him moving me toward the door with his other guests.

"Good night all," his voice sounded distant.

He stepped toward me, and I expected him to put his arm around me or at least say good-bye, but he slipped it past me instead, holding the door open. And then I found myself outside on his front porch, looking back at the yellowish outline of the light in his doorway. His form stood there in silhouette and I saw his eyes flash in anger. Then the door closed.

Blind anger filled me and then a searing pain. I was being pushed aside. What had I done wrong? He hadn't said one word directly to me all evening, and now without a single word, I was cast out into the darkness. Had I just been a toy he was now tired of? I'd thought he liked me as a person.

Tears were streaming down my face, and I was sobbing loudly.

"Hey, what's the matter?" a deep voice asked from the darkness nearby. I could tell it was Mark.

I tried to answer, but found myself clinging to him and sobbing onto his shoulder, instead. He just wrapped his arms around me and held me. Finally, he said, "It's all right. Come on with me. I'll take you home."

So, I let him lead me down the sidewalk to his car.

That night, I sank into a deep ocean of emotions I couldn't understand. I remember hearing Mark tell me he wasn't surprised at Ed's actions. "He never lets anyone get close to him. I've seen it over and over. He's the one who will hurt most in the end, though."

"I don't see how anyone can hurt any more than I do right now," I muttered.

"Let me take some of the hurt for you," he whispered, pulling me closer to him as he drove through the night-darkened streets.

When we reached his apartment, he looked at me with a question in his eyes, but I shook my head. "Please just take me home," I whispered.

I could tell he wasn't pleased, but he drove me to my small flat. As I got out of the car, he grabbed my arm, and fear shot through me. "You need to make up your mind who you really are," he said. "Either you play the game or not. But no one likes a tease."

I couldn't face seeing Ed at the bar after all this, so I quit my job there.

About a week later, I saw his car in the parking lot of my apartment complex. For an instant, my heart raced, but I took a deep breath and forced myself to relax. When I went to bed alone later that evening, I was fighting little bubbles of remorse rising to the surface of my mind. I'd let this man make a fool of me. When his car was still in the same spot in the morning, I wondered who his new toy was, and wished I could have warned her.

David called about three weeks later, bursting the bubble of self-control I'd tried to put around myself. His quiet, steady voice made me feel so guilty I was in tears before I even tried to speak. My mind refused to focus, and I felt totally unworthy of him now. I could hear his voice, but no words were registering in my mind.

"Annemarie?" he said. "Are you still there? What's wrong?"

Still no words would come. "I—David—I'm sorry." That's what I wanted to say, perhaps even thought I had said. But then I could hear him saying:

"It seems you don't want to talk to me. So, this is good-bye, I guess."

As I hung up the phone, my mind was numb. There was a vague sense of relief, but a deeper tone of regret. I knew I'd lost him, and it was all my own fault.

***

There was no way I could stand the Colorado winter after that. I contacted a high school friend who now lived in California, and said I'd like to come for a visit. The sunshine would do me good, I told myself.

Nikki said I could stay as long as I wanted to, sleeping on her couch. After a few weeks, though, I grew restless again and found a cheap motel to stay in. I sang at the bar next door, which paid enough to cover my expenses, and I kept on writing music.

It seemed my music improved, perhaps from the depths of my new experiences in pain. People seemed to find something in my songs that spoke to them, too.

And so a few years passed, as I drifted up and down the West Coast. Each place brought new faces, new people to meet, but I felt lonely anyway.

Finally, I decided to get out of the daily brightness of California sun, and headed north into the mists and mountains of Oregon.

One night, as I was singing in a small club in Portland, a stranger asked me over to his table.

"Annemarie, you have a lot of talent as a singer. But you need an agent to get you to the next level, someone to do the dirty work for you. I could do that." He handed me a business card, which read, "James Carlson, Theatrical & Music Agent."

"I guess I haven't really thought about the next level," I admitted. "I just like to reach people, and share my music with them. I *have* put a couple of my own songs on YouTube, though."

"Well, I can help you reach more people, if you want that." He smiled and added, "I like what I've heard so far."

Three or four weeks went by, and I talked to him sometimes on breaks, when he happened to be at the club.

Finally, one night, we were sitting and talking about ideas to put a song on YouTube. "This is your best song yet," he smiled.

Then to my surprise, he slipped his arm around me. As I settled back onto his shoulder, I felt warm and secure for the first time in a long time.

"You are really turning me on. How about going to a more private place?" he whispered.

"After my last set?" I said.

"Is your place close?"

"Yes, but it's nothing special, just a small studio apartment."

"Doesn't matter to me, as long as we're alone."

***

So I did what I knew I shouldn't, and became James' mistress. I convinced myself that he really loved me, and life seemed full of sunshine for awhile after that, despite the clouds and rain of Portland. James seemed to be everything I'd ever dreamed of. His eyes always spoke to me, and the sound of his deep voice would surge through my heart, filling me with more joy than I thought I could ever hold. I felt like one of the mountain streams in spring, let loose from the snow by the warmth of the sun—laughing and dancing over stones, tumbling down falls, and overflowing green banks.

I'd look deep into his blue eyes and think, 'This time I'm not just a toy. He really does care about me as a whole person. It seems too wonderful to be true, and yet it's just as real as the hillsides of trees around us, reaching up to the sky.

["Wow!" said Celestia. "You are so creative with words, Annemarie. It's like your descriptions are poetry—or songs."

Annemarie sighed, but smiled slightly. "I guess they are. I haven't thought about it much lately. It just sort of comes to me naturally."

"My mother used to write songs," Celestia said. "She hasn't for a long time now, though."

"I always wondered where I got my talent. It sure didn't seem to come from my mother."

Celestia looked into her eyes for a few moments, but then she shrugged. "I guess you'd better continue with your story now."]

Most days were like this, *[continued Annemarie]*—until winter came. Once or twice, it actually snowed, and we laughed and chased each other, throwing snowballs. But mostly, winters in Portland were wet and gray. Sometimes it rained for days on end, and gradually I found myself standing alone at my window more and more often.

My eyes would strain to focus on the wet streets below, filled with pools of light from street lamps and car headlights. On these nights, fear and uncertainty would well up inside me, the doubts I could never seem to shake.

Sometimes a week or more would pass and James didn't call or even email. I knew he would, if he could, but it made me feel so empty, not knowing. Did he really care like he had at first? Or was this just an elaborate game I'd let myself be drawn into? Then I'd hear myself asking him, "Do you really love me?"

"Of course I do, Annemarie."

Still, something inside my mind kept warning me, 'There are no guarantees here.' He was still married to someone else, for all I knew—it was something he never talked about. Oh, he mentioned his children now and then, but I really had no idea what his family life was. And I'd scold myself for getting into a relationship with a man who wouldn't, or couldn't, share his whole world with me.

On the darkest nights, I'd lie on my bed, listening to the steady pounding of the rain on the roof, and felt the same deep ache I'd felt when Ed cast me aside. Why did I keep falling into these destructive patterns? It seemed no one ever wanted all I had to give. But I couldn't let myself think of David. That still hurt too much. He was on the other side of a great chasm I had no hope of crossing now.

One day, I found myself staring into the bathroom mirror, talking to my reflection, "So what did you expect of life, a bowl of cherries?"

This sounded too trite, I knew, but my reflection didn't seem to mind. "Sometimes you just get wormy apples," I replied to myself.

"There's no such thing as a happy ending, you know," I went on. "No happily ever after—only in fairy tales."

The figure in the mirror shrugged at me. "That's a pretty pessimistic outlook."

"Well, it's true for me. Maybe there's a more sophisticated, psychoanalytical way to say it, but I don't know it."

"So now what?" my reflection asked.

"Just try to bear up and keep plugging away, I guess."

"Charge of the Light Brigade!" said the reflection, with an ironic smile. "Or maybe Pickett's Charge?"

"One of those hopeless scenarios, anyway."

I finally turned away, not wanting to continue this pointless discussion. 'Am I beginning to crack up?' I wondered, 'Talking to myself like this?' Still, maybe it was good to verbalize these feelings, even if it was only to myself. There really was only one thing to do—just keep trying to go on, in a world that would never get any better for me.

And so, I lapsed into silence. When I did see James, things seemed to be the same, but I wondered if we were both somehow pretending. I sensed some invisible wall forming between us. Had I conjured this up myself as some sort of defense? What was I afraid of? Was I causing the problem myself? All I knew was our early sunny days seemed very long ago now.

***

Portland was still in the depths of a wet winter when the call came from Chicago. James had gotten a small record company there to look at some of my videos on the Net. It was odd that I spent a lot more time thinking about my personal relationship with James than I did about my so-called singing career. Maybe I just didn't want it badly enough. But I went to Chicago, just to show myself I could do this singer-thing.

James didn't fly there with me, though. He said there was some pressing business on the West Coast he had to take care of first. I hoped it really was business and boarded the plane alone.

I'd never seen Chicago, and it took my breath away. As we approached, it was a clear day, and beyond a rim of ice along the shore, I could see the shining blue of Lake Michigan and the parks on Lakeshore Drive, just as I'd heard of it, and the tall offices and apartments lining the Magnificent Mile.

The next day, though, the Windy City clothed itself in fog. The first recording session went well, and the contract seemed very promising. But this did little to lift my spirits, there in a new city all alone. I wished I could be with James.

Was there anything wrong between us? Maybe the problem was mixing business with pleasure. Perhaps it wasn't a good idea for a client to sleep with her agent. I was afraid to come out and ask him, though. What was really worrying me, I knew, was the nagging thought he'd found someone else.

Angrily, I pushed this thought away. Of course, he had every right to. After all, there was no true commitment between us, but he was really no different than any of the other men I'd slept with. I'd just been fooling myself again.

I took a brisk walk after the session, despite the fog. Soon I found myself climbing the incline of a viaduct that went toward Lakeshore Drive. But my thoughts wouldn't so easily be left behind, like the streets behind me disappearing into the fog.

I knew the real trouble—I was always 'the other woman'. I was in love with some other woman's husband or boyfriend. It seemed I'd never be happy until I could really have a husband of my own, but who would want a used-up person like me?

My feet stopped at the crest of the viaduct's rise and my eyes turned back toward the Loop, straining to catch a glimpse of the skyline. Somewhere in this fog were some of the world's tallest buildings, but now they were completely invisible in the mists. I reflected how my early faith in God, and my love for David, had been hidden that way for many years. But now these old feelings—and regrets—were beginning to emerge, even as those skyscrapers would eventually emerge from this fog.

I turned away abruptly and walked briskly down toward the lake, not wanting to think about those buildings, or my past. Lake Michigan was eerie in the fog. I half-listened to the deep moan of a foghorn in the distance, wondering what it would be like to be on a ship in the fog—nothing to be seen around you, like you were in a dark tunnel of gray. Part of me wished I could just get on a boat and sail off into the nothingness and never have to come back.

'This lake is really a great inland sea of fresh water,' I reflected. 'Even though the horizon is lost in the mist, I can still sense the size of it. It's as though the waves lapping against the shore betray the lake—even though it tries to hide in the fog. And just like this, my thoughts are beginning to betray me.'

So, I fled again, going back to Michigan Avenue and up the massive steps of the Art Institute. There was a pair of lions guarding the doors, I saw—but they were stone, of course. I spent the rest of the day wandering the galleries, finding favorite painters like Cezanne and Monet. I'd discovered the Impressionists while in high school, so of course looking at their paintings brought back unbidden memories of those past times.

'Life seemed so much simpler then. In my innocence, I thought I'd just keep serving God. All I had to do was sing, right? But it didn't turn out that way. Where did I turn off that path? I used to think I knew right and wrong—things seemed so simple in black and white. But colors of the world seeped in and muddied the scene. Now my world is fuzzy and indistinct—just like Monet's paintings hanging before me.'

The nearest painting was getting even blurrier, and I realized tears were filling my eyes. I turned and fled the gallery, not wanting to look at any more reminders of how messed up my life was now. Was it even worth living anymore? I was wondering this much too often lately, it seemed.

***

Later, back at my hotel, I stared at my cell phone for a long time. I knew I should just send a text to James, so I wouldn't have to hear his voice. But then I thought of how Ed had dumped me without saying a word, and I couldn't do this to James. I found his number in my contact list and punched the send button.

He answered, even though I'd been hoping for his voice mail, "What's up, sweetheart?"

"Uh—hi James. I won't be back until the weekend."

"How is the session going? Do you like the contract?"

"Oh, yeah, it's all fine."

"Is anything wrong?" The concern in his voice caused my throat to tighten.

"No, I'm fine. I just have to go through Denver on my way back and tie up some loose ends."

'You're such a coward!' I said to myself, after I'd hung up.

The next thing I did was go online and re-book my return flight to have an overnight stopover in Denver. Perhaps I'd never even use the last part of the ticket to Portland.

And that's where you found me, Celestia, looking out this hotel window into the falling snow, trying to decide whether to jump or not.

"I'm not sure my timing was all that good," she sighed.

"Oh, I don't know. You kept me from jumping, at any rate."

She reached across the bed and took my hand. "What are you going to do now?"

"I really don't know. If I was strong, I'd do the right thing and break it off with James. And if I knew where to find him, I'd go to David and tell him things I should've said a long time ago. But I don't know if he'd even listen."

"You might be surprised."

"Are you an angel, or something, who can wave a wand and make things all better?" Then I stopped myself, "Oh, I didn't really mean to make my voice sound so sarcastic."

"It's okay," she shrugged. "I wish I could do that for you, but I can't. My mother made promises to yours about her life after she came back, but they didn't come to pass."

"Yeah, Mom did have a rough time, all because of me. I wish I could make it up to her somehow. But I've just turned my back on her, too. I left and never really looked back. I should have called or talked to her more."

Now the tears were flowing again, and this time I didn't even try to stop them. Celestia handed me a tissue and placed her hand gently on my arm.

CHAPTER 3

A STRANGE SURPRISE

Fog was swirling around me. Or was it the flakes of snow? I seemed to be floating with them. Had I jumped, after all? Then my feet came to rest on something solid, and I realized the swirls of snow were on the other side of a pane of glass.

With my heart pounding, I looked into Celestia's eyes and saw she sympathized with my story. "You know, I think you should meet my mother," I said.

"Well, yes, I'd like to," Celestia nodded. "In a sense, she was there when I was born—and even before, for that matter."

"Huh? How is that possible?"

"I think you'll have to ask your mother about it," sighed Celestia. "It's very complicated."

"So how do you want to get to Deer Path? Should we just drive a car or cross your GAP?"

Celestia laughed, a very musical sound. "I'm feeling really tired right now from these Time-GAPs, so think we'd better just take a groundcar. I believe you know the way?"

"Oh, yes, I know it. But there were times when I swore never to go back there."

"The memories weren't good?"

"No, not really. In a small town, when no one—including you—knows who your father is, things get unpleasant. But I'll take you. We just need to make arrangements to rent a car."

"Are you sure that's okay with you?"

I could see Celestia didn't want to put me through something too painful. "No, it's fine. I guess I'd better face my ghosts and quit running from them. After all, I'm not eighteen anymore."

And so, the next day found us driving away from a rental lot near the Denver Airport. The snow had stopped falling and most of the road was clear now. I still remembered how to drive in snow, even though I hadn't done it much for the past several years, in southern California or Oregon.

As the miles rolled beneath our wheels, I began telling Celestia more of my story:

"You know, Mom never would talk about my father. Sometimes it seemed as if no such person existed, so it got to where I gave up asking. She'd just stand there in tight-lipped silence. That was when I was old enough to ask such questions. Before, I guess I just made up my own stories. Sometimes I imagined my father was some traveling musician who she'd fallen for. After all, where did I get my love for music? It sure didn't seem to be from Mom.

"Once, I got Uncle Danny to admit her pregnancy came soon after they came back from traveling in something called the GAP with Jon and Martina, though I didn't really understand what he was talking about. And he didn't seem to have any idea who my father was, either.

"I admit once I got into high school, I'd look at my male teachers and wonder if it could be one of them. But none looked anything like me. And Mom adamantly denied it had been a teacher. I think she didn't want anyone to get in trouble over her problem.

"And as I got older, I asked her once why she hadn't given me up for adoption, like other unwed mothers I'd heard of."

"What did she say?" Celestia cut in.

"It was strange. She just shook her head and said, 'No you belonged with me. Someday, maybe we'll both find out the truth.' It was almost like she didn't even *know* who my father was, and was waiting to find out—just like me.

"That's why I finally asked her if she'd been raped. But she denied that, so I was still in the dark. I try not to blame her for the wild streak I developed after I graduated from high school. I used to think if I could just find out who my father was, then I'd know why I was like this, because I sure wasn't much like my mother. There was an angry knot deep inside me that wouldn't go away, no matter how far I tried to run."

By this time, the Front Range was gradually fading into the haze behind us. Little towns on the prairie were slipping past, most of them gone in a couple of minutes, even though I dropped the car's speed to the posted limits. And then there was the old familiar sign: "Deer Path – 5 miles."

"Well, we're almost there," I sighed.

"Are you okay?"

"Yeah. I'll be all right."

As we reached the edge of town, there was the school, still looking much like it had eight years ago when I graduated. We drove on past the water tower, the grain elevators, and crossed the railroad tracks. The little brown house on the other edge of town hadn't changed, either.

"I remember how Mom always had a bitter laugh when she talked about this house, Celestia. It was supposed to be only temporary when they moved here from Texas after the divorce. But she never moved out again. First, it was lack of money, and then I think it became lack of desire.

"After her mother, my grandma, died in this house, I think Mom couldn't bring herself to leave it. Uncle Danny had his own place of course, a few miles up the road, closer to his job in Sterling. He and his wife bought it with his share of Grandma's inheritance, but Mom just paid off the little Deer Path house and stayed there.

"Once Mom said something about why she bought this place," I said to Celestia, as I pulled the car into the gravel drive. "She said Grandma Lauren, her mother, was the only one who never condemned or judged her. 'She was a precious, loving woman,' Mom said. 'I wish I could be half the mother to you that she was to me.' But I didn't really give her a chance."

Tears were starting to come, making me angry, and I stopped talking.

Celestia could sense my tension, and placed a hand on top of mine. "We don't have to go in until you're ready," she said.

"I'm okay. All this reliving my life has made me see some things I didn't understand before. I really need to talk to Mom, too."

We got out of the car and shut the doors rather loudly, hoping Mom might hear us and come out of the house. As a matter of fact, she was standing just inside the door, when we got to the porch. She opened it even before we had a chance to knock, and pulled me into a tight hug.

"Mom, I'm sorry it's been so long."

"It's just good to see you again, Annie." Before either of us could stop it, tears were flowing, and we hugged each other even tighter.

At last Mom stepped back and turned her gaze to Celestia. "Martina?" she asked.

At this, Celestia and I smiled at each other.

"Always happens! I'm her daughter, Celestia."

"Celestia! Of course. I was there when you were born."

"That's what my mother told me," she smiled. "She and Jon both send their regards."

"It's been so very long," Mom murmured. "I thought they'd forgotten me."

"Oh, no! They've been trying to keep track of you, but many of their opportunities to communicate have broken down recently. In their time—my time—Earth is going into some terrible tribulations. That's why I came to try and find you both. Dad kept saying to wait, but I had to get to Annemarie."

At this, I elbowed her sharply, not wanting her to talk about what happened in Denver.

"Perhaps they could come *here*," Mom's voice said then, sounding hopeful.

"Not now. They have parts to play in those days of tribulation," Celestia sighed. "I do, too. But right now, I'm here because of you and Annemarie."

"Well, please come in. I shouldn't leave you out here in the cold. I seem to have forgotten my manners."

The three of us walked into the small living room and found a place to sit.

"The old couch we always started on is gone," Mom laughed.

Celestia smiled. "That's okay. I really just need to ask you some questions. Annemarie has already told me a lot of her story."

Mom looked sidelong at me.

"It wasn't pretty," I shrugged. "You know a lot of it. But I don't want to go into it again. Once was hard enough."

To my surprise, Mom gently took my hand.

"Please don't be offended," Celestia said then. "There are some questions my mother said I must ask you. You see, she and Jon have been keeping a watch over you all. You and Danny were the first people of this time they contacted. And so, they've kept up with your lives and experiences, as well as they could, to see if they've been any help—or hurt—to you. But I really need to know, when did you first discover you were pregnant?"

Mom looked at the floor a very long time before she answered. "It was just after we got back from the GAP. I'd turned seventeen. You won't believe this—no one would. But I was still a virgin, or thought I was. I never slept with anyone."

"You know, I'm told no one believed the Virgin Mary, either," I said.

"But God sent *her* an angel to explain," Mom muttered.

"And one to convince Joseph, too."

"So, you went into the Time GAP a virgin and came out pregnant?" Celestia asked.

"That's the best I remember it. You wouldn't believe how many times I've asked myself what could have happened—something that I wasn't aware of, that's for sure."

Now it was my turn to squeeze Mom's hand, trying to seem reassuring.

Celestia gave a big sigh. "I think I may know what happened. I have one more rather personal question. Did my mother, Martina, sleep with Garek, her supervisor from Salien?"

Mom's eyes grew round and wide suddenly. "You mean?"

"Better answer my question before we jump to conclusions."

"Okay. Yes, but only once. And he called her shortly after you were born, asking about what you looked like, and what color your eyes were."

"I have brown eyes like my father," said Celestia.

"Yes, you do. And Garek's eyes were blue—like Annemarie's…"

We were both staring at Celestia with open mouths now. This seemed to be a wildly impossible scenario. "Are you saying my father is some guy from the future?" I finally blurted out.

"If Ginna is telling the truth—and I have no reason

to doubt her—then it's the only explanation that makes any sense at all," Celestia began.

"Sense! It makes no sense to me."

"Wait, Annemarie," said Mom. "I wish I could explain to you what it was like to truly be 'within' someone, the way I was with Martina. I was really there, even though you could only see Martina. So I guess when Garek made love to 'us' she wasn't in her fertile cycle, but I was."

"But shouldn't I have been born before you came back—like Celestia was?"

She shook her head. "It must have something to do with the Time GAP—I think Darien called it the Einstein Effect."

"My Uncle Darien?" asked Celestia.

"Oh yes, we met him, too."

Now I was getting angry and confused. "Come on, you two! You're acting like it's some class reunion—and this is my *father* you're talking about."

Mom took my hand again. "I'm sorry. You're right. I wondered myself sometimes if this could have been what happened, but there was no way I could tell you."

"I wish you'd at least tried."

"I know. I'm really sorry."

"Now, I probably have no chance of ever meeting this stranger who fathered me."

"Actually," Celestia began, "My instructions were to bring you both back with me, if you're willing to come."

Mom's eyes brightened for the first time. "To think that after all these years—I'm over forty years old—of going back, or rather forward, again."

"How old are you now, Annemarie?" asked Celestia.

"Twenty-five."

"Well that all fits. And you're sure, Ginna?"

She nodded.

"I guess. Mom couldn't have made this up. I never dreamed of such a thing."

"Okay. I can take you both, since I'm firstborn. I don't know if your ages will change when we cross the GAP. All that compensation stuff gets confusing to me sometimes. But I will keep you safe. And if Garek is to be found, we'll take you to him."

"We?" said Mom.

"My parents and I," Celestia nodded.

"Oh, it will be so good to see Martina again."

By this time, Celestia got out the amber lamp and set it up on the coffee table.

"Yes, Jon always set it there," said Mom.

"Dad told me the lamp makes it easier to cross big Time-GAPs."

Again, the lamp seemed to produce its own power source, as lights of many colors began to circle and swirl on the walls of the living room.

CHAPTER 4

INTO THE FUTURE

Ginna wasn't sure where they'd ended up. The lands around them looked dark and bleak, not at all like the Earth she remembered, either from her own Twenty-first Century or from Martina's time. It looked like the fields around them had been scorched with fire, and many of the buildings on the horizon were leaning at strange angles.

"Oh, dear," Celestia cried, "Things here are worse than when I left."

"Can't you take us to some other time?" asked Annemarie.

"Not really. These are the only coordinates I have for locating my parents," she sighed.

Ginna was shading her eyes and scanning the horizon. "That shoreline seems familiar," she said at last, pointing toward a large lake to their left.

"Well, it's a start," nodded Celestia. "I think that's Omato."

She set off toward the blue on the horizon, with the other two women following closely behind her. As they walked, the fields around them gradually shifted their colors from the black of scorched earth, to the drab gray of stubble fields that hadn't been planted for a season or two.

"I seem to remember this all being lush and green," said Ginna.

"There've been too many battles here in recent years," Celestia said.

"Who's been fighting?" asked Annemarie.

"Oh, just about everyone. First the System attacked the Rebels here. Then the Rebels retaliated. After that, people from the overcrowded eastern landmasses poured in, looking for food and shelter. But instead of finding any grain, they torched what little was left."

"Why would they do that?"

"I don't know, Ginna. Desperate people do things that don't make sense sometimes."

"Well, none of this makes any sense to me."

"Please, Annemarie, just try to be patient," Ginna sighed.

"I'm sorry, Mom. I'm just confused. I've never time-traveled before like you."

Celestia cut in, "Oh, that's right. We'll try to help you more. It does take awhile to adjust to the GAP-crossing for some."

As they neared the lakeshore, they began to make out a tall buff-colored cliff to their right. There were only a few scraggly trees growing at its base, and the bastions of rock seemed to rise abruptly above them. Ginna wondered whether she'd be able to climb these cliffs as well as the younger women could.

Celestia stopped and looked intently at the cliff-face. Suddenly she seemed to recognize something. "There it is."

"There what is?" Annemarie asked.

"The cleft my mother told me about." She pointed, and the other two tried to make out what she was indicating.

Ginna could see a slight shadow which perhaps wasn't entirely natural, but Annemarie shrugged, "I don't see anything."

"Come on anyway," Celestia called over her shoulder, as she turned and started toward one of the steepest parts of the cliff.

"Are you sure you know where you're going?" Annemarie called after her.

Celestia's only answer was to motion with her arm for them to follow.

Just then a loud screeching sound filled the air, and they instinctively covered their ears.

"Lie down!" shouted Celestia. "Get as flat as you can on the ground."

Ginna and Annemarie dropped together, clinging to each other. A strong gust of air passed over them, and the sound of rushing wings filled their ears.

"What was that?" cried her daughter, beginning to sit up.

"No, stay down!" came Celestia's voice. "It's circling back around."

This time full-blown terror gripped Ginna, and she found herself trying to burrow into the hard, dry ground beneath her. She could sense some menacing hot breath across her back, but didn't know if it was something biological or mechanical.

Gradually the heat receded, and then she heard a scuttling sound. At first, she felt panic again, until she saw Celestia crawling toward them out of the corner of her eye.

"What was that?" she asked.

"One of the System's Robo-raptors," replied Celestia.

"Is it gone?"

"I'm not sure."

They lay there on the bare ground for a few more minutes. Finally, Celestia said, "Let's make a run for the cliffs. Are you ready?"

She and Annemarie each took a deep breath and nodded.

As one, the three of them jumped to their feet and began to run as fast as they could toward the bastion of rock.

Off in the distance, there was a dark shape circling in the white-hot sky. It looked like an eagle, but something wasn't quite right. Then, as it turned and began to move closer to them, Ginna saw it was five-times larger than any eagle she'd ever seen. Its eyes were flaming red, and its fierce, hooked beak was larger than its head.

"Is it a machine or a bird?" she asked Celestia, breathlessly.

"Both!" Celestia didn't seem to have much breath to speak either. "If it gets any closer, lie flat again. Otherwise, keep running."

They tried to watch and run at the same time, but all they could do was concentrate on putting one foot in front of the other.

"I thought the System denied the existence of Earth," Ginna panted.

"Are we still on Earth?"

"Yes, Annemarie. I can't cross GAPs between planets without a ship." Now Celestia stopped and bent down, trying to catch her breath. "For some reason, the System has 'rediscovered' us."

Just as she finished speaking, the Robo-raptor swooped low over them again, leaving them groveling in terror. Then a long, low whistle sounded in the distance, and the creature banked and flew away toward this new sound.

"Quickly! Make a dash for the cliffs." cried Celestia. "Something has distracted it."

As they got closer to the upthrusting rocks, it did seem there was a long vertical crack beginning to take shape out of the shadows on the wall. When Celestia reached the base of this crack, she kicked at some reddish boulders nearby.

To their surprise, a smoothly-cut step appeared, as one of the boulders tipped away. Celestia led them up this step, and as they turned a slight corner to the left, another step appeared. Once they climbed up this, another smooth step appeared, and then another. Soon they were moving deep into the side of the cliff and could no longer see any-thing of the plain.

All were out of breath by the time they reached a level spot. "Almost there," Celestia called.

Now there was a sound of dripping water just above them. Up a few more steps, and they could see a small stream trickling down a smooth face of rock to their right. Celestia stopped briefly at this and touched her hand to the water. "Blessed be the Living Water," she whispered.

"The water that comes from the Rock," Ginna added.

Annemarie turned toward her mother and said, "That sounds like something in the Bible."

"I think it's from The Book," smiled Celestia.

"Same thing," said Ginna. "*Byblos* means *Book* in Greek."

By now Celestia was already around a corner ahead of them, so they pressed on. It wouldn't do to lose her now.

A little farther on, the sound of moving water became louder. Around another turn in the path through the cliff, and they were facing a wall of crashing water.

"A waterfall?"

"Sure is, dear," said Ginna.

"So how do we get past this?"

"We don't," laughed Celestia. Then she ducked into a small hollow place in the rock wall behind her, leading them into a long narrow tunnel.

At last, as they emerged from this tunnel, Ginna saw a small lantern burning. The smell of the oil in the lamp seemed to hit her in the face.

Celestia wrinkled her nose. "Is that moose oil?" she asked, directing her question to a blank wall.

"We have to make do with what we can get," said a voice.

Then a figure with dark hair emerged from the shadows.

"Martina!" Ginna cried.

"Is that you, Ginna?" The voice moved closer.

"Yes, it's me." She and the slightly taller figure moved into a tight embrace.

"I never thought I'd see you again," said Martina.

"Well, I kept hoping," Ginna replied. "I tried every way I could to call you."

"You know it doesn't work that way."

"Yeah, but I was so lonely for you."

"I'm sorry, Ginna. For everything. We were really trying to help, but it seems we somehow hurt you instead."

"No, don't say that," Ginna said.

Then Martina turned toward her daughter. "So, were our guesses correct?"

"It seems like it," Celestia nodded.

"Now what do we do?"

"I'm not sure, Mom," said Celestia. "But there will be no keeping any more secrets from Dad, will there?"

"No, I have to finally face my consequences," sighed Martina.

With this, Celestia took Annemarie by the hand and moved her closer to Martina. "This is Annemarie, Ginna's daughter," she said.

Annemarie gazed into the face that looked a lot like Celestia's. Their hair and the shape of the face were much alike, but Martina's eyes were very green, instead of her daughter's deep brown.

Martina took one look at Annemarie and gasped. "You do have Garek's eyes! In fact, you look so much like him that it scares me." Then she grabbed Ginna's hand. "I'm so sorry! I had no idea this would happen."

Ginna found her mind whirling with conflicting thoughts. Part of her wanted to reassure Martina it was all right—that she knew they'd meant no harm to her. But the past twenty-six years of her life had been mostly hell-on-earth, first because of all the stares and whispers of people in Deer Path, and then because of her daughter's rebellion. There seemed to be no end to the heartaches.

She found all she could do was squeeze Martina's hand and stare silently at her own daughter, as though she were a stranger to her now.

"I'm glad you got here ahead of Jon," whispered Martina. "I'd like to explain this to him in private first."

"Explain what to me in private?" came a deeper voice from the hollow behind them.

"Oh!" Martina jerked her hand up to her mouth.

"Is that Celestia's voice I heard?"

"Yes, Jon. She's here, and she brought some visitors."

"I know," his voice echoed in the cave. "I saw them escape from the Robo-raptor. Fortunately, it followed my decoy sound."

Then he stepped into the small room, ducking his head so as not to hit it on the roof. Celestia grabbed him in a tight embrace. "So it was you! Thanks, Dad."

He smiled at her, and then turned to look at her companions. "Ginna!" he exclaimed. "So Celestia did find you." Then he turned curious eyes on Annemarie.

"This is my daughter," Ginna whispered.

"Yes, I can see it in the shape of her face. But her eyes are so blue."

"Honey, I need to talk to you." Martina pulled him aside. "Celestia will take care of our guests." She nodded to their daughter.

Ginna looked at Martina questioningly, silently asking if she should follow them. But Martina shook her head, and led Jon through a smaller doorway near the back of the cave. The three women were left standing awkwardly, trying not to stare after the couple.

Then Celestia led them through another small opening in the opposite end of the cave. They followed, thankful they wouldn't have to hear Martina and Jon's conversation.

There was another smelly moose-oil lamp sitting on a flat stone in the center of the small room they entered. Celestia began to build a small cooking fire in a fire-pit near the lamp. Ginna helped by handing her pieces of kindling, and then gradually adding larger pieces.

Annemarie seemed uncomfortable, and just watched.

Suddenly there came a sound like someone sobbing loudly in the distance. Ginna and Celestia exchanged fearful glances, and then looked toward Annemarie, who muttered, "Don't look at me like it's my fault. I didn't cause this." But as soon as she saw Ginna's eyes, she looked down and added, "I'm sorry, Mom."

The sobbing gradually faded away, and there were indistinct murmurs. Then these, too, faded into the background sounds of water dripping, and the distant waterfall rumbling.

They ate some dried meat Celestia boiled for them in a small pot, with some green and orange chopped vegetables thrown in. Ginna smiled when she tasted it, saying,

"It's a lot like the berry-leather stew Jon used to make in the Far Wilds."

"I guess it's one of his old recipes," Celestia shrugged. "Though the plants here aren't the same as on Terres, he always says."

"Maybe it's just the taste of something cooked over a campfire," Annemarie said.

"Probably. You know, I'm not sure why I never took you camping."

"I guess we just got too busy."

Ginna nodded. But she didn't share any of the other thoughts creeping into her mind, like how camping might have reminded her too much of the time she was 'within' Martina—or of her own childhood.

Celestia now brought out some coarsely-woven blankets. Without saying much, she banked the fire, and curled up into the blanket she spread close to it. "You may sleep anywhere you can find in here that's comfortable," she said.

Ginna settled herself a little further from the fire, wondering if she needed to be careful of any sparks reaching her blanket. The others didn't seem very concerned about this, so she curled up and tried to will herself to sleep.

"You know," she said, "It *is* strange how all this feels familiar—like I've already been here before."

"Maybe since you were 'inside' my mother before, it comes back to you."

"That must be it."

***

Annemarie lay on the blanket for a long time, trying to get comfortable on the hard floor. Sleep eluded her. 'It would do no good to tell the others I'd rather not be here at all. Mom seems to think it's important to find this Garek, but I'm not sure it's a good idea. Does this person really exist? Or is he a phantom she just dreamed up? How can this weird theory she and Celestia tell really be true? I'm afraid this will only lead to more disappointment.'

She must have finally dozed for a little while, for the next thing she knew there were two other figures huddled by the dim coals of the fire.

"I'm so sorry, Jon," said one of the figures. She knew it was Martina's voice.

"I don't know what to think," came Jon's voice. "How could you keep this affair of yours a secret all these years?"

"Well, once I knew for sure Celestia was yours, nothing else seemed to matter. I really just forgot about him."

"Did you *really?*"

"Yes," Martina sighed. "How can I make you believe me?"

There was a long silence. When Jon didn't answer, Martina's voice finally went on:

"Dear Jon, you've always been my rock. Your love is

what saved me from the bondage I'd fallen into on Terres. But at first, I felt totally unworthy. I didn't see how you could really love me. No one ever just loved me for 'me'. When you finally convinced me that you cared, and when we found the cleansing of the Fountain in the Desert—well, everything from the past didn't seem to matter anymore. I had no idea my actions could affect Ginna the way they did."

Then came another long silence, but she could see Jon put his arm around Martina's shoulders. "None of us had any idea such a thing would happen," he said at last. "But what do we do now?"

"I feel we owe it to Ginna and Annemarie to try to find Garek."

"What good will that do?"

"Well, for one thing, Annemarie has a right to finally meet her father. And I think Garek should know he has a daughter."

"I guess you're right. I wonder what his reaction will be?" he mused.

"I do, too."

"If we can find him."

'Yeah,' thought Annemarie. 'That's a really big IF.'

CHAPTER 5

THROUGH GINNA'S EYES

I woke slowly, feeling the aches in my joints, not a comforting feeling because it reminded me I wasn't getting any younger. As usual, this led to thoughts of how none of my life had gone as I'd hoped:

When Danny and I first come back from being 'within' Jael and Martina, I felt a deep emptiness inside, like a part of me was missing. We'd spent several years in their future time, experiencing many things, both good and bad. And yet, we'd returned to our little house in Deer Path, Colorado on the same night we left it.

When Jon first took us, I'd been fearful of participating in this experiment of his. What would it be like to live someone else's life, inside their body? Would my own self be lost? Or would I feel like a person with a split personality?

Neither of these were accurate descriptions, I soon learned. I could see what Martina saw, think her thoughts, and yet there were still some thoughts of my own some-times bubbling to the surface. At times, we even were able to communicate with each other. The strangest part was how I began to feel what she felt, whether it was happiness or sadness—any emotion. At times like these, I did feel as though I was disappearing as a separate person. But this wasn't a bad thing. I began to enjoy 'being' Martina.

The strongest feelings we shared were love and fear. When Jon, through no fault of his own, crashed our spaceship on Platius, I knew all the terror. And when we reached the hospital in Urbis, I felt the fear that Jael and Jon wouldn't survive their injuries. This unleashed a love for Jon. Like Martina, I was terrified of losing the dearest people to me in the Galaxy.

This is where it got complicated. I think the Ginna-part of me fell in love with Jon at that time. Martina must have felt it, too, for this was when she finally began to realize she did reciprocate Jon's love for her. Before that, she hadn't been able to believe anyone could really love her for herself. So perhaps it was because of my 'feelings' she grew in her attraction to Jon.

All this caused some confusion for me, though. When we finally found Earth, Martina and Jon eventually got married, and then I became hyper-aware of every sensa-tion, and I knew I was 'really there'—in a greater sense than I could ever explain in words. I never 'talked' to Martina about this, however. How could I explain I was as much 'partnered' with Jon as she was—perhaps even more than she was?

And still, somehow, I also was attracted to Garek, when that affair began. He was, in some ways, the kind of man I'd always dreamed of marrying. His gentle strength, his caring way of listening to other people's thoughts, his joy in life—all of these drew me to him. And again, I think perhaps I was even more taken with him than Martina was.

I'm not sure, but I wonder if my emotions were stronger because I hadn't made love to any man before 'entering' Martina. She had, however, as she freely admitted. In the Terres Underground and later with the Redlarks, she was many a man's plaything. And maybe this was why I became pregnant by Garek, if that was what had really happened.

When they brought us through the GAP again, to our own time, it seemed no time had passed on our Earth. This was like the first time, when Jon and Jael took us with them, but this second return was much more difficult for me. Danny was very fond of Jael and missed him for a long time. But for me, it was like a part of myself was ripped away.

I'd *been* there, intimately, as Martina went through all her turmoil—of deciding whether to go with Garek, or stay with Jon—of trying to follow God's will for her life, and also seeking redemption for all the sins we both knew she'd committed. I'd been there when she made love to both these men, and I was there when Celestia was born nine months later.

Martina's question was answered by the fact that Jon had the dominant gene for brown eyes, and Garek didn't, so Celestia's brown eyes could only have come from Jon.

Then, after I was back in my own time and place, I discovered *I* was pregnant. I was in shock, with no idea what to do. Like Martina, I wondered for nine months who was the father of the baby growing inside me.

Soon my mother could see the evidence I kept trying to hide. She sat me down one day.

"I can tell you're pregnant." She came right out with it. There was no denying none of my jeans were fitting right by this time. "Who is the father?"

I shook my head and tried to think of an answer to that unanswerable question. "I don't know."

"And why not?" Her voice came more sharply now. "How many men have you slept with?"

"In this century, none."

"What is that supposed to mean, young lady?"

By this time tears were beginning to fill my eyes.

She suddenly pulled me into a hug, and the tone of her voice changed. "Oh, Ginna! Are you telling me someone raped you?"

I just nodded then. How could I possibly tell her I'd been in the future? She'd never believe such a story. And then, to add I'd come back pregnant and didn't really know for sure how? Or when? Suddenly, I remembered how I'd wanted to warn her against having an affair with her boss—not so long ago. The tables were sure turned on me now.

"But who, when?"

There she was, asking the two questions I myself couldn't answer. So, I just cried all the harder on her shoulder.

"Cry if it helps," she whispered, smoothing my hair with her hand. "Maybe someday we can sort this out."

I nodded, sincerely hoping some of this would make sense someday.

From then on, Mom and I drew much closer. She supported me in my decision to keep the baby, and she was always there for me when the emotions, and later the work of raising a child alone, became too much for me.

Still, sometimes it was a waking-nightmare. And then Mom discovered the lump in her breast when Annemarie was five. We were both devastated. She fought the cancer for four more years, so at least she got to see a few more of her granddaughter's growing-up years. She also got a good lawyer to make sure all her estate was in order, so we could have a home when she was gone. Things were still tight financially, especially with all her medical bills, but we just kept on as best we could.

Danny also did his best to help, but soon he had a

family of his own to care for. He took the job in Sterling so he could stay closer to us, I think. I'm sure he'd gotten better offers in faraway places.

As Annemarie grew, her love for music became more and more obvious. When I bought her a guitar, she was thrilled, and began to teach herself to play it right away. Listening to her playing and singing reminded me of Darien and his manitar. And Martina had played the flute, I remembered. Then I also realized Garek had said his daughter was a talented musician. This, and the bright blue of Annemarie's eyes, made me stop and think. Could Garek possibly be her father? Had time warped when we crossed the GAP, so my pregnancy was delayed, while Martina's wasn't?

Many a night, I tossed and turned, wondering if it was even possible, but this was way beyond my comprehension, and there was absolutely no one I could ever explain it to. They'd think I was going crazy. On these nights, I was almost glad Mom was gone, because I might have tried to tell all this to her, and she would've thought I'd totally lost it.

So I never told anyone, and tried to just put it out of my mind. It was the only way to keep on living day to day.

Things seemed to go well for Annemarie up through high school. I knew some of the kids in town talked about her behind her back, so I tried to share how Danny and I felt when we'd been bullied in school. She seemed to turn to God for strength, which I was glad of, and I was especially happy when she and David began a relationship.

But it seemed nothing good could last in my life. David left her behind with a promise ring when he went away to college. Then she suddenly seemed to turn angry and rebellious—and moved with her guitar to Denver, deciding to try a career in music. I knew she and David were too young to marry, but part of me wished they had.

These were the years when she seemed to put me off. It would be weeks or months, sometimes, before I heard from her. I kept telling myself this was just another stage she was going through, as she tried to find a place in a world which seemed against her from the start. And I told myself she didn't realize she was breaking my heart.

Then she and Celestia turned up in a rental car, in my own driveway. For the first time in a long time, it seemed one of my prayers had been answered.

So here I was, curled up in a blanket, on the floor of a damp cave—somewhere in the future—and this time I was seeing things through my own eyes, alone.

CHAPTER 6

THE SEARCH BEGINS

Dawn didn't reach into the cave, so I had no idea whether it was day or night the next time I awoke. Martina and Celestia were tending a small fire. On a spit over it, some medium-sized animal was roasting. Even though I had no idea what it was, it did smell appetizing.

"Good morning," I mumbled. "*Is* it morning?"

"Yes, Ginna, it is," Martina smiled over at me. More than twenty years had passed since I was 'within' her, but there seemed to still be a kind of intimacy between us not expressed in words. We weren't in each other's heads, like before, but we did seem to be able to understand each other's thoughts.

"Yes, the sun is up. Jon's gone out scouting."

I noticed she stopped there, not giving me any information about what—or who—he was scouting for. Or any information on where we were.

Celestia continued slowly turning the spit on which

the meat was roasting. And I could see my daughter still sleeping in her blanket nearby.

"I'm wondering if you know where Garek is." I decided it was better to just put this out there now.

Martina stole a sharp glance at Celestia. "No. But Jon is trying to find out what he can."

"Hey, don't get mad at Celestia for telling me everything," I said. "This is something I've been mulling over in my mind for more than twenty-five years."

"Then you did suspect?" asked Martina.

"I couldn't think of any other explanation."

"I wish I'd thought of it." Martina reached over and took my hand in hers. "I just got caught up in living my own life, and forgot about Garek—and you. Can you forgive me for that?"

I took a deep breath before answering this. "I can't say I'm happy about your forgetting me. After all, you'd promised me that living my own life would be better than staying in you."

She nodded silently at these words, and I could see tears forming in her eyes.

"Still, it was the life God planned for me. And there were sweet things along with the bitter." I glanced at Annemarie's sleeping form as I said this.

Just then there came a rustling sound at the cave's doorway, and Jon stepped in. He was wearing a heavier jacket than yesterday, and it seemed to be damp.

"It's gotten colder out there," he said, brushing at the sleeves of his coat and setting down a heavy-looking packsack beside him. "The rain is beginning to change to snow."

Martina stepped over and kissed him on the cheek. "Any luck?"

"I did get some news of Darien's group."

"I hope Jael is still with him," she sighed.

"The Rover I met didn't know one way or the other."

"How far is it to their Safe-Zone?"

"It sounds like a long day's journey in good weather. And, fortunately, it's to the west, so we'll be sheltered by the forest—from things like Robo-raptors. We'll have to wait for the snow to let up, though."

Celestia let out a disappointed moan at this news. "Stupid snow."

This woke Annemarie, and she sat up abruptly, rubbing her eyes. "Snow?"

"Well, I did get something to soften the blow," Jon said, pushing the packsack toward his daughter. "Darien sent this for us."

Celestia's face brightened quickly as she began taking stock of the contents of the bag. "Wow! Look at this—real flour and sugar. And even some tins of fruit. Gosh, it's been a long time since I had juicy canned fruit."

"You should've told us to bring some of this stuff," I said. "I have a pantry full of canned goods."

"Thanks for the offer, Ginna," said Martina, turning toward me again. "But we can't take edible supplies from your time across the GAP."

"Why not?"

"We're not really sure," Jon replied. "It has something to do with things that were once alive being adversely affected by the time-jump. Whenever we've tried it, the food spoils, and becomes inedible."

"But when we went to Tornatoh, we took food with us," I mused.

"That wasn't a full time-jump, just a space one," said Jon.

Meanwhile, my daughter crawled out of her blanket and began helping Celestia sort through the food from the pack. "This looks so yummy." She held up a colorfully labeled tin.

"Pick out one to open for breakfast," said Martina to her daughter.

"I'd like the figs," she replied. "Is that okay with you, Annemarie?"

"Sure! I haven't eaten figs for years."

Soon, all five of us were gathered around the firepit, munching on canned figs, while the meat on the spit began to brown. The fire let out spluttering sounds as drips of grease landed in it. When the figs were gone, Jon carefully took the meat off the spit, successfully burning his fingers in the process.

"Ouch!" he cried once or twice, sticking a finger into his mouth.

Soon, the meat was torn into five fairly equal pieces, and we began to chew on our share.

"Uhm, what animal is this?" I finally asked, after my first few bites didn't provide any revelation.

"Ground hog," said Jon, between bites.

This answer caused me to hold my piece away from my mouth as I stared at it, wrinkling my nose.

"Sometimes it's better not to ask," chuckled Martina.

"I guess so," I mumbled. "I've learned my lesson. If it tastes all right, don't ask."

I finished my piece despite my misgivings. All the meat was soon gone, and only bones were left. Jon and Martina began sucking the marrow out of these, too.

"You should try this," she nodded to me. "The marrow is the best part."

"I'm full for now," I shrugged.

"If you're sure," she said. "Okay if I take your bones, too?"

I pushed them toward her.

"You really should try it, Ginna," said Jon. "The marrow has some of the best nutrition."

By this time, Martina had broken one of my larger leftover bones in half. "Here try it," she insisted. "Just suck on the end."

So I finally did, and admitted the slightly greasy

marrow did taste pretty good, especially if I closed my eyes and didn't see where it was coming from.

"Mmm, it *is* good!" I heard Annemarie say.

"Why do I feel like a caveman?" I mused, still sucking on the other half of the bone Martina had broken. "I thought we were in the future."

Jon laughed at this. "I can see it seeming strange to you. But this is what most Believers and Rebels are reduced to in our time. We've been cast out of all the cities and cut off from any trade."

"Why is that?"

"Well, every time there's a battle or a war," said Martina, "The Powers in charge find a way to put the blame on us, even though we didn't cause it. The more the planets in and out of the System keep fighting with each other, the worse life gets for us."

"The Rebels do fight when they're forced to," Jon added. "Eventually we'll all have to take our stand—for or against the True King."

"Why doesn't the King come back to Earth to fight alongside his followers?" Celestia asked.

"There is a time when he will." Jon nodded toward his daughter. "Only he—or rather, his Father—knows when the time is ripe, though. Right now is when the storm clouds are just beginning to gather."

"And all we get to do is wait—and try not to starve," she moaned.

"Come on, Celestia, it's not that bad."

"Maybe not for you, Dad. You have Mom, but I get lonely."

I knew what she meant, and so did Jon apparently because he began to blush, the redness starting in his ears and slowly moving into his face. He turned away toward the fire, pretending to stir it.

None of us seemed to know what to say next. Finally, Martina broke the silence, "So how long do you think this snow will last, Jon?"

He shrugged and turned back to face us. "Hopefully we can set out tomorrow or the next day."

I heard Celestia and Annemarie moan at this, and had to admit the thought of staying cooped up in this cave for two more days didn't appeal to me either.

"Perhaps the girls and I could do some tracking lessons while you check your trapline, Jon."

He nodded at this, and began to smile again. "Sounds like a fine idea, Martina."

Then he turned to smile at me, and I could feel my heart trying to rise into my throat. Quickly, I looked down. Apparently, some of my old feelings for Jon had survived all these years. I wondered how I would feel if I ever got to see Garek again.

*****

The snow was just over ankle-deep under the eaves of the forest, and I worked to keep pace with the others. Annemarie and Celestia were right behind Martina, and I kept putting one foot in front of the other, watching the footprints as I did so. Martina's stride was a bit longer than mine, so it was more effort. But it seemed easier to put my feet into the depressions her boots made than to break my own trail.

Besides, I didn't want to accidentally step out of our path and mar any tracks we might find. Looking up again, I saw the other three stopped, staring intently at the ground.

"Did you find some?" I asked, coming up with them, and trying not to sound too out of breath.

I could see Martina smile at me—it seemed she knew how hard I was working. My daughter also seemed to be out of breath, so that made me feel better.

"Looks like a small rabbit was here," Martina said. She was pointing to some strange-looking marks in the snow. In the front were two oblong depressions, with smaller round ones right behind.

"Rabbits hop, so their hind feet land in front of their forefeet," Celestia explained.

Stepping gingerly, trying not to disturb the area, we followed the trail. Suddenly it ended, and there were feathery hand-like imprints over the tracks.

"What's that?" Annemarie asked.

"Looks like a hawk or an owl swooped down and got some dinner," replied Martina. "Those are its wing-prints."

"Oh, the poor bunny," I sighed.

"That's just the way of the wilds," she said softly. "I wonder if things will be different when the True Lord establishes his new Earth."

"What on Earth are you talking about?" my daughter demanded.

"It's in the book of *Isaiah*," said Martina. "It talks about the lion and the lamb lying down together, about children putting their hands into poisonous snakes' holes and not being bitten. It says, nothing will kill or destroy in all the land."

"Well, that sure isn't what Nature's like now," I said.

"Then it *will* really be something new," said Celestia. "I can hardly wait to see it."

"I wonder how long until it comes," I sighed.

"Don't forget, The Book says no one knows the day or the hour," Martina reminded us.

We all stared in silence at the scene of the rabbit's demise. Then Martina motioned for us to follow her again.

Soon we could see small hoof-marks in the snow. Sometimes they were set in a fairly straight line, and then they would seem to cluster randomly.

"The deer have been nibbling a lot on this shrub." She pointed to an area with many milling tracks. "See how they've bitten off the tips of all these branches."

I could see that virtually every branch on the shrub before us was nipped. "Will it kill the bush?" I asked.

"Hopefully not," Martina smiled. "It depends on what kind of shrub it is, and whether it will sprout from its roots. This one probably won't make it, though." She pointed to a small tree nearby with long strips of bark missing, pale bare wood showing all the way around the stem. Higher up on the trunk there was another bare spot.

"What happened here?" asked my daughter.

"A young buck probably rubbed the velvet off his antlers here. See how the bark is torn off?"

"Velvet? What's that?"

"When deer first grow their new antlers each spring, they're covered with a velvety brown coating," said Martina. "It's actually a sort of skin which supplies circulation to the antlers as they're growing. Once the deer's antlers are grown to that year's size, the velvet begins to slough off. It must be kind of itchy because the deer are always rubbing their antlers against something until the velvet is all worn off."

"Wow! I had no idea," said Annemarie.

"Do deer grow new antlers every spring?"

"Sure do, Ginna," nodded Celestia. "And each year they add another point, so the new antlers are bigger than the ones they shed the winter before."

"So, a deer with a large rack of antlers is older than one with a small one?"

"Usually, Annemarie," she replied. "Of course, only males—the bucks—have antlers."

Just then, Annemarie pointed to a large depression in the snow, a few steps off our deer trail. "What's that?"

"It looks like a deer bedded down there," said Martina. "Taking a rest."

"Whew! I'm glad it wasn't some other animal killing the deer."

"Well, that does happen," Martina nodded. "But there'd be more signs of a struggle, and probably some bones left over, especially if it was a wolf kill."

"You mean there are wolves here?" I tried to keep the fear out of my voice. "We didn't have those in Colorado."

"Yes," there are wolves in the wild places now," said Celestia. "They were reintroduced into some wilderness areas back at the end of the Twentieth Century."

"That's my time." I was surprised at this.

"They repopulated better than anyone expected," Martina added. "And now, with all the wars, more places have gone wild again, and the wolves just keep multiplying."

"As long as they have a food supply," Celestia put in.

Despite myself, I could feel my skin getting gooseflesh and tried not to think of the old stories I'd heard as a child about "The Big Bad Wolf." I felt as though my ears were listening for a distant howl.

Martina shrugged though, and said, "We haven't found any wolf tracks around here recently."

"AHoooo!" came a sudden call from the thicket to our right.

My daughter and I nearly jumped out of our skins.

"That's just my dad," laughed Celestia. "He always howls when he's gotten something in one of his snares. Let's go see what he caught this time."

She and Martina set off at a brisk pace toward the source of the sound. I tried to calm my racing heart as Annemarie and I followed them. Soon we could see a bit of green and blue against the grays and browns of the trees. Then we made out Jon's form in a plaid shirt.

"What did you get?" called Martina.

"A couple of nice fat rabbits," he called back, "And this…"

We caught up just as he was holding up a furry dog-like form. "Is that a wolf?" I asked.

"No, too small," he chuckled. "It's a coyote. Did you see any wolf sign?"

"No. We were just talking about them though, so we have wolves on the brain," Celestia laughed.

"I have one more snare to check," he said. "Down by the river. Want to come?"

"Sure," I nodded.

"I think we three should take your rabbits back and start some dinner," said Martina.

Jon smiled and handed the rabbits and the coyote to his wife and daughter.

"Will we eat the coyote?" I asked.

"Probably not," said Martina. "Carnivores' meat tends to be very strong in flavor. But maybe I can manage a stew."

"Keep the pelt," said Jon. "I know it will be handy."

"Oh, I intend to," Martina smiled.

"Okay. We'll see you at the cave," Jon added. "We won't be long."

As Jon and I trudged through the snow toward the sound of trickling water, I tried to breathe in the cool crisp smell of the winter forest. "This is a beautiful place."

He turned and smiled at me. "Yes, it is—especially on this side of the cliffs, where more rain comes, and the vegetation is thicker. It's safer here, too—more places to hide. But most of the time, I'm too busy trying to find food for us, so I can't really enjoy it."

We walked on several more steps in silence. "I'm glad you came back with Celestia," he said suddenly.

"Why?"

"Well, Martina has been wondering about how you were doing, and your daughter, too, of course. But now that I've seen her—well the blue eyes make it clear she's not mine."

His voice tapered off into silence. I wondered whether I should say the words in my mind. Then I just shrugged and decided to be brave and just let it out, "I've been wondering about all this for over twenty-five years. But you know, two brown-eyed people can have a blue-eyed child, if they both carry the recessive gene. So she could be yours..."

"I guess I've heard that," he said softly. Suddenly he grabbed my hand and pulled me into an awkward hug. "We never meant to hurt you, honestly."

"I know." I was trying not to let him see the tears forming in my eyes.

He did though, and began to wipe them with a gloved hand.

"Please," I murmured, pulling away from him. "I can't—"

"What?"

"Please don't put so much temptation in front of me. I've always loved you, Jon. But you're Martina's."

He stepped back in surprise, his eyes looking into mine.

"It happened when I was 'inside' her, I guess. I felt everything she did—and once I was myself again, I realized that I loved you, too."

"But Annemarie is Garek's—you think? Martina seems to think she resembles him. I've never met him."

"He's the only other possibility. I never had sex with anyone else but him—and you—when I was 'within' Martina."

There, I'd said it all in plain words. He frowned a little, but then stepped closer to me again.

"You know, I do care a lot for you, Ginna. But you're right. Martina is my one true love. I think I knew it from the first time I saw her in the Redlarks' camp."

"And that was before I was 'inside' her. You know, I hope we *can* find Garek," I finally admitted. "I want to know if there are any feelings in either of us. I think there might be—because I still have feelings for you, after all these years, so maybe I will for Garek, too."

"I've often wondered what Martina actually felt for him. She never really says."

"I think her feelings were mixed," I shrugged. "I've begun to think it was because of *me* that she was attracted to him."

"Well, that's an interesting thought. Then I wonder who *Garek* was more attracted to—Martina or you?"

"I guess only he can answer that."

Just then we reached the edge of the small river. The banks were lined with ice, with billowy piles of snow on top. Then they dropped off to dark icy water, gurgling as it flowed along the ice's edges. "Careful, Ginna, the ice can give way and you'll get wet feet."

I held back as he stepped carefully along the bank, looking for his snare. Suddenly he gave a whistle and then his usual howl.

"What is it?" I asked.

"Looks like I got a beaver."

I came up to where I could look over his shoulder.

Right at the edge of the water, his snare held a brown animal with long, thick fur, and a large flat tail. "Definitely a beaver," I smiled.

"You do know something about wildlife, don't you?"

"Well, I spent much of my life in Colorado, in the mountains."

He was grinning now. "This should make a great stew. I can hardly wait to show Martina."

As soon as he got the animal out of the trap, he slit the belly lengthwise, taking out the entrails. These he tossed into the forest, and then slung the beaver over his shoulder, hanging it by a loop of rope he'd tied around the forepaws. And so, the two of us trudged back up to the crest of the ridge, and made our way toward the cave in the cliff above us.

Once back in the cave, we could smell the appetizing scent of rabbit stew. In a nook where light from the door reached inside the cave, Celestia was showing Annemarie how to skin the coyote and prepare the pelt.

As I stepped close to them, she looked up at me and grinned. "I'm trying to learn some survival skills, Mom."

"I hope we won't have to use these particular skills in our time," I said softly.

"We all do what we must," said Martina, coming up behind me.

"How do you manage?" I asked her.

"Well, after we were evicted from the cities, we learned to survive as best we could. There are a few small Rebel Safe-Zones, like my brother Darien's, with large enough shelters to farm for numbers of people and help small out-claves, like us. They even have some basic manufacturing in the larger underground caves, especially the ones in the eastern mountains. But the more food we can get for ourselves, and the fewer goods we take, the more there is for others."

"How many Believers are there left?"

"No one knows for sure, because not all the out-claves communicate with anyone," Martina said. "There are just the three of us here."

"Now five," added Celestia.

"Yes, five—and there are probably a hundred in Darien's Safe-Zone."

As she added us to her tally, I suddenly realized we were a big liability for them—two more mouths to feed. Now I knew how much Martina and Jon cared about my daughter and me, to take us in during these desperate times in their own lives. I tried to think of some words to tell them how I felt, but couldn't find any that were adequate. Instead I grabbed Martina's hand and squeezed it.

She looked at me, and there was a light in her green eyes telling me she'd received my wordless message. Perhaps some of our old 'oneness' still lived in each of our minds.

"Come on, girls," she said suddenly. "Let's get this stew into our bellies. I know I sure need it."

As we gathered around the firepit, Jon pulled Martina and me toward him, taking one of our hands in each of his. Celestia brought Annemarie into the circle, and Jon said a prayer of thanks for our meal. "And thank you also for having our friends with us again. May we always seek to do your will."

"Amen," said Martina.

"Amen," I echoed.

The smoke from the cooking fire made my eyes smart, but I knew better than to ask why it was so far from the cave entrance. There was a slight hole in the ceiling above it, small enough that no light could leak out into the potentially hostile world outside.

For a few minutes, no one said anything as we scooped stew from the ceramic bowls Martina handed us. I kept blowing on each spoonful, wanting to take the food in quickly, but trying not to burn my tongue.

"Do you think the weather will break tomorrow, Jon?" Martina finally asked.

"The sunset seemed pinker tonight," he nodded. "That usually means a dry day to come."

"Red sky at night, sailor's delight," my daughter recited.

"I've heard that, too," I said. "The rest says, 'Red sky at morning, sailors take warning.' "

"If that's true, we should hope for no red in the sunrise." Jon said, smiling up at me.

I let my eyes drop quickly, so he wouldn't see how they longed to gaze into his.

Once the stew was all consumed, Martina began scrubbing out the pot. Instead of washing it with soap and water, she rubbed it clean with a piece of stone, and then wiped it with an oiled cloth. I was watching closely, when she looked up and caught my eye.

"This is better for the pot than soap and water," she smiled. "It keeps it seasoned well, and we save the soap for other washing."

"I guess you do whatever works," I shrugged.

"That's for sure."

"Here, let me try."

"You can clean out the bowls. I use this smaller stone for them."

When we finished scrubbing the dishes and set them in a hollow space in the cave wall, I reflected how life seemed easier when there weren't so many possessions to take care of.

"You know, Martina, I was just thinking sometimes our possessions take possession of us."

"How do you mean, Ginna?"

"Well, you don't have a lot of stuff to take care of, so life seems simpler. Less cluttered."

Her face clouded for an instant. "We live this life out of necessity, not by choice," she frowned. "But you know, maybe it *is* a blessing in disguise." She took my hand in hers. "Thanks for sharing that with me, Ginna."

Her eyes brightened a bit, and I smiled into them, "I want to do whatever I can to help you, Martina."

During this time, Jon was showing Annemarie and Celestia how to pack what we'd need for the hike to Darien's Zone. When we finished putting the dishes away, we went to join them.

"If this was Terres," he was telling them, "We'd have berry-leather and bark packsacks. But here we make do with smoked meat, and hopefully a bit of fruit-leather."

"There are still a few dried blueberries," Martina said, handing him a bag she pulled from a small cubbyhole nearby.

"So that's where you hid them," he teased.

"You knew good and well they were in there," she laughed. "I just didn't remind you."

"Until you needed to. I know."

Watching them together like this made my heart ache, but I tried to put these thoughts out of my mind. After all, hadn't I made it this long without ever knowing the love of a man, or knowing if my daughter's father even knew she existed? But it was almost impossible to swallow the lump rising into my throat.

"Okay, Mom," Annemarie said somewhere nearby, "I've got you some extra warm clothes packed, and your share of the food."

"Thanks, Honey." I smiled at her across the open packsack.

"I think we should all get some rest now," said Jon. "We'll need to set out at first light."

As I lay on my mat for our second night in the cave, I found sleep eluding me, so I lay quietly on my back, hoping not to disturb anyone. Above my head somewhere, was a quiet dripping sound as some underground water seeped its way into the cave. I wondered whether some of the snow would be melted by morning.

Somehow that sound of water suddenly took me back, and I was sitting beside a campfire with Dad, looking out at a grassy field on a summer night. I must have been only ten years old—the divorce came when I was nearly twelve. I hadn't seen him much after that, and we'd never gone camping again.

The next feelings came in an instant, like a sharp hunger pang. Tears sprang to my eyes, as my whole being longed to feel the heavy, cozy heat of a sultry southern night. My eyes saw the flash of lightning bugs springing into view and then fading out, as they flew at random in the grass before us. I reached to take Daddy's hand, but mine closed on empty air.

The tears welled out of my eyelids and trickled down my face, into my ears. I knew the scene I'd see tomorrow was the sparkles of snow-reflected light, not the light of fireflies. And I knew my father had been lost to me a long time ago. I'd grown used to the aloneness. But now I hoped perhaps Annemarie would get to see *her* father, at least once.

CHAPTER 7

INTO THE ZONE

We set out at first light. Martina and Jon came to bed late. I heard them talking about getting the coyote and beaver meat put into a cold area of the cave, to preserve them until we were able to come back and prepare them properly. Again, I was feeling guilty, because we were a burden to them here. But I knew neither of them would ever say that.

The snow ended during the night, and the air was crisp and cold. As we walked, our breath came out in billows of steam. And as I expected, the sunlight made the snow crystals sparkle like tiny diamonds scattered on the white ground.

No one talked much as we trudged through the snow-filled forest. Occasionally, we saw a vista of hills and valleys when an opening came in the trees. As the sun grew warmer, trees began to drop their burdens of snow. Sometimes a limbful would land just in front of one of us—or even cascade down onto someone's head. At least this gave us a few moments of comic relief.

Jon stopped us in the lee of a hill just as the sun seemed to be reaching its zenith.

"Let's take a lunch break." He smiled at Annemarie, who was closest to him.

"So what gourmet delight do we have today?" she laughed.

"How about fruit-leather?" said Martina.

"Somehow, I think I've tasted that before," I chuckled.

"But that was on Terres," Jon said. "This is made from Earth fruits."

By this time, he'd broken off a chunk of the flat, dry leather for each of us. Chewing it was a familiar sensation, even if the taste was slightly different than the berry-leather we'd eaten during our trek across the Far Wilds of Terres, so long ago.

I thought if I closed my eyes, I could almost feel what it had been like then—leaving everything any of us knew and setting out with our only goal to find a better way to live than on Terres. I was 'within' Martina then, and Danny had 'become' Jael. Jon was our guide, just like he was now.

Inadvertently, I glanced over at Martina and noticed her eyes were glued to me.

"You feel it, too, don't you?" she said.

I just nodded, afraid if I spoke my voice might break, and the tears would come.

"I just hope this journey turns out as well as that one did," she sighed.

Again, all I could do was nod.

"What journey?" asked Annemarie.

Fortunately, Martina had an answer, "Oh, your mother and I are just remembering a journey we took together long ago."

"The one to the Fountain in the Desert?"

"Well that was where we got eventually. But I was remembering the very start," I found myself murmuring, "When we first set out into the Far Wilds of Terres."

Jon looked up in surprise. "You still remember all that?"

"Of course, dear," Martina smiled. "It was a pretty vivid time in my life."

"Mine, too," I shrugged.

Jon just looked from one to the other of us and blinked.

"We're grateful for all you did on that journey, Jon," said Martina.

His eyes flashed suddenly, and I wondered what he was remembering, but was afraid to ask. Part of that journey—for him—had been about learning to love Martina as more than a High Chieftain's Consort. And for Martina (and me), it involved coming to terms with feeling worthy of Jon's love.

Also, for all of us, it was an odyssey of finding the truth

about the Lord of the Universe. That part was successful, thankfully, for we learned what it meant to belong to this Lord, and be cleansed body and soul by the Fountain.

My mind began to drift then, and I tried to keep my thoughts from going the direction I knew they would. 'I sure wish Jon was Annemarie's father.' There my thoughts had said it. Now, hopefully, I could just put it out of my mind.

Once we finished gnawing on our fruit-leather, we stood and stretched. My knees were aching after sitting, and I hoped they'd feel better once we got moving again. Then we each shouldered our packsack and set out.

As soon as we began to move through the trees again, I had a strange sense we were being watched. Nervously, I glanced toward the sky, wondering if any Robo-raptors could spot us down here in the forest.

Then suddenly, there came a low grunting sound, mingled with a squeal, and the brush crashed and swayed off to my right. Quickly, Jon stepped between us and the sounds.

"What is it?" Martina barely whispered.

"Wild boar," he hissed. "Nobody move."

Now I could see a large, black shape standing among the trees, staring at us with evil-looking, yellow eyes.

"What can we do, Dad?"

"I'm hoping he'll be satisfied with some dried meat and fruit-leather," murmured Jon. "Take my pack off very slowly."

"How about if I just pull the food out while it's still on your back?"

"If you think you can."

"Sure, I can. I'm taller than you now, you know."

The slightest bit of a smile in her voice helped to ease my tension a bit.

As quietly as she could, Celestia began easing packets of food out of her father's packsack.

"Take it all," he whispered. "We need to keep him busy as long as we can."

Once the food was out, she gave about half of it to Jon, and he nodded to her.

Now I could see the boar stepping slowly out of the trees. He was huge and covered with coarse black hair. His head seemed to occupy a full third of his body. Along his neck, stiff hairs bristled up in a sort of mane. The tusks protruding from his mouth looked like fearsome weapons. I could feel my blood run cold at the sight of him, even though he was still fifty meters away, staring at us with glowing red eyes.

"Okay," said Jon softly. "When we throw the food, back off slowly. Try to skirt around to the left as quietly as you can. If he charges, get as high as you can into a tree."

My heart sank at this. I'd never been a good tree-climber. By now my knees were quivering, and I wasn't sure I could even move without falling on my face.

In a sudden movement, Celestia and Jon threw the

food packets toward the boar. One nearly hit his snout. He gave a squeal and seemed about to charge, but then he caught scent of the food, and began tearing into the packets.

We moved back, as Jon motioned to us, and gradually swung far to the left of the boar. He was making ghastly sounds as he ripped through the food packets.

After what seemed like eternity, we were past him, and the sounds finally faded into the distance.

"Was that another of the System's mutant animals?" I asked at last, when I could breathe again.

"No," sighed Jon. "They aren't Robos. But someone's been breeding the fiercer Eurasian boars with the smaller North American species.

"I seem to remember reading some game animal breeders were secretly doing that back in my time," I said.

"Well, perhaps they've restarted the experiment, or these could be the descendants of your time," Martina added.

"At any rate," said Jon, "You've just met the most dangerous animal in the wilds—more dangerous than bears, cougars—"

"Or even wolves," his daughter cut in.

"Individually, at least," he nodded. "But a pack of wolves is nothing to trifle with, either."

"Could the System start breeding these as attack drones?" I asked, "Like the Robo-raptors?"

"We haven't heard of it yet, but it's possible," he shrugged.

"They seem fierce enough, as it is," added Annemarie.

"I think we'd better step up the pace, Jon," Martina cut in. "We don't want to be out here when night falls."

He nodded silently, and took her hand. We all walked much closer together after this.

The afternoon was warmer than the morning. The sun continued to cause trees to drop their loads of snow, and soon icicles were dripping and sending water rivulets onto our heads, too. Trees became sparser and smaller, and soon we reached the edge of a grassy prairie. In the distance, we could see grazing animals like horses or cattle.

As we got closer, we found our guesses were correct. Some of the horses raised their heads when they sensed our approach and whinnied to us. One of the larger horses—a black and white pinto—seemed to have a rider. The figure waved and shouted a greeting.

"It's Jael!" Martina cried. She began to dash in his direction as the horse galloped toward her.

Soon he was on the ground, and he and his sister were embracing, laughing and crying all at the same time.

After a few minutes of conversation, Jael finally looked up at me. "Is that you, Ginna?" he cried.

I barely had time to nod, before he locked me in a strong embrace. "Yes, but don't choke me," I laughed.

"You seem to have finally regained all the strength you lost in the crash on Platius."

"Oh, yes," he chuckled. Then he looked at me quizzically.

"I was there, too, you know."

"Oh, that's right. You were, weren't you?"

Then his gaze turned to Annemarie.

"This is my daughter, Annemarie," I said.

His eyes were full of questions, but he was too polite to ask them just then. Instead he nodded to her, "Very pleased to meet you."

"Why don't you ride ahead and tell Darien we're coming," Martina said then, to break an awkward silence.

"Sure," he smiled. "My horse can carry two. Who wants a ride?"

"I think I may need one," I said quietly. "My knees are protesting about all this walking."

Jael helped boost me onto the painted horse's back. Holding tightly to his waist, I hoped I wouldn't embarrass myself by falling off.

"This is my own horse," he nodded as we started off at an easy lope. "His name is Splash."

"Splash?"

"Yeah," he chuckled. "He looks like someone splashed him with black and white paint. How is Danny doing?"

"He's doing very well. He and his wife, Sandra, have two wonderful boys, and they still live in Colorado."

"I think of him often."

"He thinks of you a lot, too, Jael."

Soon we'd left the others several meters behind us. Now that we were out of earshot, Jael apparently had to ask his questions.

"So, were you ever married, in your own time?"

"No. And I know what your next question will be."

"Where did Annemarie come from?"

I sighed. "That's the question everyone asks me eventually. And the answer is, I don't know for sure. When you took Danny and me back, I discovered I was pregnant. I never married anyone, and I'm still not sure who her father is."

"You mean you think she was conceived here?"

I began to feel embarrassed as Jael—who was still a boy in my mind—asked these intimate questions, but felt I needed to explain myself, so I continued, "That's the only possibility, because I never had relations with anyone after you took us back to our time."

"Really?"

"Really."

Silence crept between us then.

At last, I had to break it. "Do you believe me?"

"Sure, I do."

"The only possibilities are Jon and Garek."

"Oh, yeah, Garek. Martina mentioned him once or twice. Wasn't he her supervisor in Salien?"

"That's where I 'met' him, so to speak."

"But you aren't sure?" By the tone of his voice, I could tell he didn't know about his sister's affair.

In light of this, all I could think of to say was, "Well, Martina and Jon seem to think her father is Garek, because of her blue eyes. But I—or your sister and I—only slept with him once."

I was glad we crested a small hill then, and I could stop talking. There before us were several huts made of sod, with thatched roofs. Jael gave a shrill whistle, and a willowy red-haired woman stepped out of the nearest one.

"Jael!" she cried. "Who have you brought?"

"Is that Raina?" I asked.

"Sure is." He jumped off the horse and lead it by the halter, with me holding on to the mane for dear life.

Raina dashed over to him and planted a kiss on his lips. "I'm glad you're safe," she said. "There were some System Patrols in the area."

"I'm fine, Honey," he said, holding her close to him. "Look who I've brought—Ginna."

Raina shaded her eyes from the sun as she looked up at me. "Really? Wow, it's great to meet you, Ginna. Jael and Martina have talked about you often."

"Martina and Jon are coming along behind." As he spoke, he walked toward their hut, with me still on the horse behind them.

"Uh—how do I get off this horse?"

Jael laughed. "Here!" Then he reached up, and helped me slide off the pinto's back.

As my feet touched the ground, I felt something warm nudge the middle of my back. Turning, I was surprised to come face-to-face with Splash.

"I think he likes you, Ginna," Jael chuckled.

Even as he said this, the horse nodded and huffed. Then he nuzzled my shoulder. I wasn't sure what to do, so I just patted the black and white face gently. Splash's warm breath felt moist on my hand.

"There are the others," Raina said just then, and we all turned to see the four others striding over a distant rise. "Who's that with them?" she asked as Splash nickered and moved away from us to munch on some grass near the hut.

"That's my daughter, Annemarie," I said, glancing at Jael. He just shrugged, his way of letting me know it was up to me to explain or not.

A sense of relief flooded me at this. At least for now, I didn't have to admit I had no idea who my own daughter's father was.

Just then, a slender boy erupted from the door of the hut. "Daddy!" he cried, throwing himself into Jael's arms.

"Hi Jace. How's my boy?"

Watching them brought a smile to my face, and then tears to my eyes. It was a long time since I'd been able to hug my Daddy, or a child, for that matter.

"Here Jace," said Jael. "This is Ginna, a friend I've known for a very long time."

The boy nodded his blond head in my direction, with the casual air of an early teen-ager.

"Hello Jace," I nodded. "How old are you?"

"I'm twelve Earth-years," he said, shading his eyes and looking up at me.

"Please come inside, and I'll get us all some tea," said Raina, motioning me toward the door.

We stepped through the low doorway, and when we were joined by the others, settled on some upturned boxes which appeared to serve as chairs around a small firepit. Soon each of us held a steaming cup in our hands. The tea seemed to warm my whole body as it slid down my throat.

"What kind of tea is this, Raina?" I asked.

"It's a mixture of catmint and chamomile," she replied.

"It really hits the spot," said Jon.

"Is Darien in camp, Jael?" Martina asked.

"Yes. He's meeting with the Elders right now. He should be free by suppertime, though."

"Good," Jon nodded. "We need his help with a little project." He glanced at me as he said this, and I knew I was that project.

CHAPTER 8

ANOTHER KIND OF SEARCH

"I really don't know what to say, Ginna," said Darien. "We have so little contact with the cities anymore. And it could jeopardize our security to let you go out searching for this fellow Garek. Our best defense right now is lying low."

I was looking down at my hands, as he said this. The last thing I wanted was for my problems to cause trouble for others. I'd lived with them this long, so what did it matter? That's what I was trying to tell myself, but I knew it wasn't true.

Glancing over at my daughter, I could see her eyes flaring with emotion. It was even harder for her to hear there might be no way to find her father.

Celestia seemed to sense what Annemarie was feeling, for she took her hand and rubbed the palm of it with her thumb. My throat constricted at this. I could remember how it felt when Jon did this for Martina. My own hands were almost tingling at the touch that wasn't there.

"What about a Net-search?" Celestia asked. "Could we at least try?"

I saw Martina nodding in agreement. After she'd explained our situation to her brother, she'd been sitting in silence.

Darien turned to look into his niece's eyes. "Why does this mean so much?"

"Try to imagine how Annemarie must feel, Uncle," she said. "She's lived her whole life having no idea who her father is. And now we've come all this way, only to learn we can't even search."

Jon glanced at his daughter, and when he spoke there was tension in his voice, "I know how it feels to suddenly learn the person you thought was your father—isn't." Now it was Martina's turn to take his hand. "My mother told me on her deathbed."

His voice choked off as he tried to hide the strength of his emotions. I found I did remember the story he finally told us one night, as we sat around a small campfire in the Far Wilds—of how his mother was seduced as a young woman on Rubicon, and then cast aside when her lover found she was carrying his child. Later, Jakol, the man Jon had known as father, took her in and raised the boy-child as his own.

Now Darien looked each of us in the eye briefly, and I could see his manner begin to soften. I remembered him as a strong and decisive commander of Rebel Forces, and I knew from Martina how this brother of hers tended to be moody at times. Jael was steadier, but Martina had some of Darien's characteristics. I wondered what their dead brother, Stephen, had been like, but all I knew were indistinct glimpses I'd gleaned from Martina's mind, all those years ago when I was 'within' her.

"Celestia, I'll let you begin a Net-search. But please keep to the security protocols I give you," Darien said at last.

"Thank you, Uncle," she beamed. "We'll do whatever you say."

With that, Darien nodded to one of the guards at the door of his office, which was in one of the two brick buildings in the compound. The man stepped forward and led the two young women out. Then Darien turned to his sister and spoke, "Would you like to see Mother?"

"She's here?" Martina gasped.

"Yes, we managed to spirit her out of the city last week."

Martina leaped to her feet, almost dancing with joy.

"Calm down, Sis," he smiled. "She's been very ill. It was a risk to take her away from where she could get medical care, but—well—she wanted to be with us when the end came."

Martina froze in mid-step at these words. Now her hand went to her face as she gasped, "Oh, I didn't know. Why didn't you tell me?"

"We only found out a few days ago, after my messenger was already sent to Jon. When he reported back, I knew you were coming. Otherwise, I would've sent word."

Jon had risen by this time, and was holding Martina around her waist. "We understand, Darien. There's only so much we can do with communications in these times. May I take Martina to see Irina?"

Darien nodded, but didn't speak. I began to wonder if he was also trying to fight back emotions, like his sister. At last, he said, "She's in the Infirmary—fourth building on your right, as you go out this door."

Once they'd gone, I found myself alone with Darien, groping for something to say. He seemed to be trying to pull himself back together.

"I'm sorry about your mother," I whispered.

"We've had twenty more years with her than we ever expected," he said then.

I nodded, remembering the joy Martina felt at their reunion in Celeton, when we'd returned from the Fountain in the Desert, and learned Irina, Raina, Daiah, and Dominic had managed to escape Terres, and find their way to Earth.

"I've seen Raina. How are the others?"

"Dominic recovered well from his injuries in the blast at Alpha Centauri. He and his son Dom are serving at another Safe-Zone. Daiah is now my wife." He started to smile as he said this.

"That's wonderful!"

"Yes, we've been blessed. She's come to be a Believer, and we have a son and a daughter."

I smiled, seeing the love and joy in his eyes. "What about the others?"

"You mean Jakob and Myra?"

"Yes, I didn't really know them well—we left so soon after that reunion."

"They were well the last I knew. They're manning an outpost near the Fountain in the Desert."

"How far is it to the Fountain from here?"

"Several days' trekking, since we have no groundcars anymore. And it's across some very dangerous ground."

"I wasn't thinking of going there," I smiled. "I've been once."

"Ah yes, with Martina."

"More like 'in' her."

"I never did understand that. It seems impossible to comprehend."

"Well, I experienced it, and I still don't comprehend it fully."

"And you think this Garek—that my sister slept with—could have—"

"Yes, they seem to think I somehow got pregnant."

I was blushing crimson by this time. It was getting difficult to discuss this with all these comparative strangers. And the part I kept to myself—wondering if it actually could have been Jon who had produced my daughter in me—how could I possibly reveal these thoughts?

"Well, I hope we can help you and your daughter learn *something* about all this," he sighed. "I need to go to a debriefing now." He rose and strode toward the door. "Is there anything I can get for you?"

"No, thanks. Could you just show me where Celestia and Annemarie are?"

He nodded and gestured for me to precede him through the doorway. "The Netlink is in the third building to your left," he pointed.

"Thank you, Darien." I set off in that direction, and he went the other way, toward a long brick building in the center of the compound.

The heavy door was hard to open, but I finally managed it. At a desk inside, the two girls were hunched over a keyboard and a small screen. Annemarie looked up as she heard me close the door behind me.

"Hi, Mom."

"Any luck?"

"Not much," said Celestia. "There are a lot of Garek Carsons out there. Who would've thought it was such a common name?"

"Mom, do you know what his middle name was?"

I tried to think, but nothing came to me. "I'm lucky to even remember his surname," I sighed. "Sorry."

"Let's try by location," Celestia continued. "We know he was working in Salien about twenty-five years ago."

"You know," I said, "I wonder how all this time shifting might affect the future—uh, I mean, your future, Celestia."

"Yeah. How can we know we won't do something, just by being here, that changes your future?"

"Well, I don't know," Celestia shrugged. "Perhaps there *is* no way to know. We started down a different time-line the moment I brought you here."

"I wonder what else changed when Jon brought Danny and me here before."

"I guess we have to hope some force greater than us is controlling our lives," sighed Annemarie.

"Dad tells me that's what he believes."

"You mean the True Lord of the Universe, Celestia?" I asked.

"Mom, is that who we call God?"

I nodded. "We're just like tiny bugs—or even less—if you look at the vastness of the Universe."

The two of them fell silent then, knowing I'd seen some of the infinite expanse of space when Danny and I traveled with Jon, Martina, and Jael. Just then the keyboard gave a chiming sound, and a new screen popped up.

"Hey look, Mom. I think we found something."

There on the screen was a name in bold letters, "***Garek C. Carson, Forestry Commission, Salien.***"

"I think that's him," I said, actually feeling more excitement than dread.

"It gives two other addresses," said Celestia. "It looks like he may be in Tornatoh now. But that's a long journey from here."

"Can't we cross the GAP?" I asked. "That's what your father did when we went there looking for the Fountain."

"I'll have to ask him," she nodded. "And also, it will have to be cleared by Uncle Darien and his Elders."

I nodded and tried to smile at them. There was no way of knowing if the ones in charge here would approve of such a trip in these treacherous times.

***

Not long after we found the location of Garek, Martina and Jon walked through the door behind us. I could see worry in her eyes, and Jon was holding her close.

"How is your mother?" I asked quietly.

"She said she feels better today," Jon replied.

Martina just nodded.

"Have you found anything?" Jon walked over to the terminal screen, glancing over Celestia's shoulder.

His daughter pointed to the notation we'd found on the screen, showing Garek Carson now resided in Tornatoh. "Do you think we could cross a GAP to get there, Dad?"

Jon shook his head. "I don't know if the Elders will approve."

"Can't you try to convince them—please, Dad? This is really important to Annemarie."

I was watching my daughter's face, as Celestia talked. She didn't seem nearly as intense about this as Martina's daughter did. Why had Celestia taken this on as something important to her? It wasn't her father we were looking for. Had something passed between them before they came to get me in Deer Path?

Martina was still standing near the door, so I walked over and took her hand. A grateful look came to her face, and she drew me out the door with her. The last rays of daylight sun were falling on the ground between the huts. Without speaking, the two of us just walked, still hand-in-hand.

"Are you okay, Martina?"

She nodded, but didn't speak.

At last, we stopped near the edge of the compound where a log stockade wall rose, blocking our way. "I guess we'd better not cross this right now," she sighed.

"What's wrong with Irina?"

"She's aging prematurely—probably because of the powerful drugs they gave her at the Institute on Terres. We can be grateful she's still with us, though. Jon's mother wasn't so lucky."

"I guess the disaster of the double-star was actually a blessing for her," I tried to smile.

Martina turned and looked into my eyes. "You're right.

I never thought of it that way. Without the disaster—and Raina—we would never have seen her again at all."

"I guess even things seeming terrible at the time can turn out for good."

"Yes, I keep forgetting that, Ginna."

"There's a verse in The Book which says, 'And we know that in all things God works for the good of those who love him.' "

"Really, where is that?"

"It's in the book called *Romans*," I said. A long silence settled over us, and we walked back toward the hut where we knew Jael and Raina lived.

"Ginna?"

"What?"

"Do you believe that *all* things work together for good?"

"I try to, even though it isn't always easy to see how they will."

"Like your getting pregnant because of me?"

"Martina, please don't beat yourself up about this. What happened—is—well, just what happened. Having Annemarie hasn't been all bad. The Lord has brought some good out of it already—I have a daughter who loves me."

I stopped then because the tears in my voice were making my throat close up.

"Our daughters *are* a blessing, aren't they?" she added, patting my arm.

I nodded my head, but didn't trust my voice to speak.

***

After this, a few more days passed. I tried to be patient, but inside I was restless. If I had to face Garek in the flesh to meet some need in my daughter, then I wanted it over and done with.

Somehow, Jael must have sensed my tension, for he took me out every afternoon to Splash's pasture. At first, I just petted the pinto's nose. But soon, Jael showed me how to brush and curry him. Then, the third day he coaxed me into riding him bareback.

I'd ridden horses a bit with friends back home in Colorado, but those had saddles and bridles.

"This is really different," I said, as Jael smiled up at me from the ground. He was still stroking Splash's mane.

"Don't worry," he said. "He's used to this. Just use your knees to guide him."

"But I'm using my knees to hang on, Jael."

He just smiled, stepped back, and gave the horse a pat on the rump.

I bounced up and down as Splash trotted around the grassy field. Then he began to lope faster, and I grabbed for his mane. But when he shifted into a gallop, I finally found the rhythm of his strides and began to move with him instead of against him.

As we passed Jael again—for the third or fourth time—I even managed to return his smile.

"Whenever you're ready to stop, just say 'Whoa'," he called.

By now I was beginning to feel exhilarated, so I passed Jael a couple more times before I let my legs dangle a bit lower and shouted, "Whoa, Splash!"

The horse slowed to a stop right by Jael. "Good job, Ginna," he grinned.

"Can we do this tomorrow, too?"

"Anytime you want, Ginna."

After this, the days didn't seem to crawl by. I had something to do besides sit around and wait.

After a couple more days, Jael and Raina took us at sunset to the brick building in the center of the compound.

"Everyone gathers here once a week," Jael said.

"Yes," Raina added. "It's a time for us to be together, to talk about our faith in the True King, and to support one another. We just call it 'The Gathering'."

"Like the church services we have back home," I said, looking over at my daughter. Silently, I was wondering how long it was since she'd been in a church.

"I guess," Raina shrugged. "I've never been to your time."

"There are similarities," Jael said, and I knew he was drawing on memories from Danny, when they'd been 'together.'

There were several benches arranged in two semi-circles in the large central room. Most of them were full when we walked in, so we ended up taking the front-most seats.

"This is just like home," Annemarie smiled. I tried not to giggle that people still didn't like to be in the front of the room, even in this distant future.

Darien saw us enter and moved over to join us. Daiah stayed in her seat, but nodded to me and smiled. Beside her were two teenaged children, both with dark hair and blue eyes like hers. I began to realize how good it was to be back here with people who knew me, in a sense, and somehow understood.

Looking around, I noticed the lights in the room came from tall white candles. As I reflected more on this, it made sense. At least they smelled better than moose oil lamps. Then I thought that if someone were to ask me what skills a person might need in the future, I would tell them, 'Learn how to make candles.' Some might call it one of the oldest professions known to man—finding a way to have light in dark places.

A gray-haired man moved to a small podium at the center of the room. Opening a large copy of The Book, he read, " 'The Lord is not slow in keeping his promises, as some understand slowness. He is patient with you, not wanting anyone to perish, but everyone to come to repentance.' *Second Peter, chapter 3, verse 9.*

"Tonight, we meditate on the Lord's patience," he

said, closing The Book. "Some of us have waited much longer than we ever imagined for his Second Coming. Some of you thought you'd never live to see your children born—let alone your grandchildren. And yet, here we are.

"We must not give up hope. The Lord warned us of this temptation thousands of years ago in this very same book of *Peter*. He warned that there would be those who scoff at us, call us crazy—try to beat, scare, or force our faith out of us—saying, 'Where is he? Nothing ever changes. He's not coming.'

"But they deliberately forget the times the True Lord has worked in the past, the ways he has preserved his people through many different trials. They don't believe these words we read are anything more than myths. But, in our hearts, we know differently.

"We know his Word is true, 'And we have the word of the prophets made more certain, and you will do well to pay attention to it, as to a light shining in a dark place, until the day dawns and the morning star rises in your hearts.' *Second Peter, chapter 1, verse 19.*"

His voice stopped then, and he bowed his head.

"Lord, we pray you will keep us firm in you," a voice said behind me.

"Lord, help us keep looking forward to the new heaven and new earth you've promised," came another voice.

I found my mind turning back to the vision Martina

and I had seen of Heaven when we went to the Fountain in the Desert.

"We have so much to look forward to," Jon's voice rang out loud and strong, and I knew he was remembering the same vision.

Then I heard a familiar voice begin to sing. It was my daughter:

"Some bright morning when this life is o'er,
I'll fly away—to a home on God's celestial shore,
I'll fly away. . ."

I joined in, and then several others did, too:
"I'll fly away, oh glory, I'll fly away;
When I die, hallelujah, by and by, I'll fly away."

Nearly half an hour later, we were moving toward a large table spread with plates of bread, fruit, and vegetables. Near one end were large pitchers of a red liquid of some kind.

"Welcome to our Agape Meal," said Darien. "This is our time to share love and food, the way the Lord did with his disciples long ago."

"Sort of like our Communion," I said.

"Exactly," Martina nodded. By the tone of her voice, I knew she'd gleaned this from my own memories.

I found myself standing beside Jon and Martina as

they handed pieces of bread and fruit to each other. "The idea is to give food to each other," she said. "Not just take it for ourselves."

After watching them for a few minutes, I picked up some grape-like fruits and handed one to Martina. Then I turned and gave one to Jon. His eyes caught mine, and he smiled. I looked down quickly, so as not to betray my feelings for him again. Glancing around, I saw Annemarie and Celestia exchanging some carrot-like vegetables. I decided to take a piece of bread to Daiah.

"Hello, Ginna," she smiled. "It's good to see you."

"This is probably the first time you've seen me in my own body," I grinned.

"I guess so. But still, I sense the same person I met before, except that now you're yourself alone."

"You know, I wondered how it would seem to others when Martina and I were around."

"Well, I'm perhaps more empathic than some," she said. "Darien tells me I sense things he can't."

Her eyes wandered the room, finding her children. "Come, I'll introduce you, Ginna."

I could see her eyes in both of them. They also had the dark hair she and Darien shared, though her son's was wavy like hers, while the daughter's was straight. "Ginna, this is my daughter, Alexia," she said. I smiled at the young girl who reminded me a great deal of Irina, her paternal grandmother.

"Hello, Ginna," she said politely. "It's good to have you here."

"Thanks."

"And this is my son, Andre. Andre, this is Ginna, a friend of your father's."

"More like of your Aunt Martina's," I added.

"Pleased to meet you," he said, and shook my hand. "Mother, may we go see what Jace is doing?"

"Yes," said Daiah. "But be home before the last bell."

He nodded and took his sister's elbow. Soon they were off in a corner with their cousin.

"They're so polite," I said.

"They can be when they have to," she laughed. "And they know when to stay on my good side, if they want to cut short the Meal and go play with Jace."

"How old are they?"

"Alexia is nearly thirteen, and Andre is eleven."

"Wow! Those are almost the exact ages Danny and I were the first time Jon and Jael came to us." I found myself reflecting on events dimmed with age, but now they seemed to jump back into my mind, sharp and clear.

"I'm glad Jace is here," Daiah was saying. "It helps to have family close with times being so hard now."

"I can see that." I was only half-listening to her, though, as I watched my daughter and Celestia. "I wonder what those two are up to." I nodded toward them.

"Hmm," she said. "Perhaps they're just getting better acquainted."

The two were sitting on a small bench in the far corner of the room, heads together, whispering. Then Annemarie looked up, caught my eye, and waved. I raised my hand and returned her smile. "Well, it's not as though we can hover over them," I sighed. "They're both adults now."

"I have to admit, I prefer my children being young right now," said Daiah. "I worry enough about them as it is, but at least I'm still the boss, you know?"

"I know Celestia has mentioned there are tribulations now. What kind of dangers are there?"

"Well, hostile Patrols and disguised Drones are some. It's never good to leave the compound in groups smaller than five—and always keep your eyes and ears open for unusual insects and birds."

"Like Robo-raptors?"

"Yes, but there are tiny insect-sized Drones, too."

I shook my head. "I'm surprised you're not scared out of your wits."

She smiled. "We just keep on trying to trust the Lord to protect us. Growing our own food is complicated, too. We must keep the fields small and close-by. I don't know what we'll do when our clothes wear out. I guess I'll just have to keep patching them. The children wear mostly hand-me-downs."

"How do you get power to run lights, terminals, and such?"

"We have a small wind turbine, and the power is

stored in fuel cells. But we get by with candles as much as we can."

"I noticed that in the Gathering. So, the candles aren't just for atmosphere?"

Daiah laughed aloud at this. "No, not really."

"Come to think of it, when times get tough, the candles always come out. In my time, there would be power blackouts."

"Yes, we had those often in the cities. Seems someone always found a way to blame those on Believers."

"You're kidding?"

"Oh no, we became the scapegoats for anything and everything that went wrong, even though we were the ones trying to live the most simply, not depleting the planet's limited resources. Still, the Powers found ways to marginalize and then ostracize us."

I nodded silently. Looking back at my own time, the early Twenty-first Century, I could see where these things had their beginnings.

"Would you like to stay in our hut tonight, Ginna?"

"Are you sure it's okay?"

"Yeah, it's better if we spread the five of you out, since our huts are so small."

"I see. It's easier to find room for one or two than for five."

"You've gotten the idea," Daiah smiled. "One would think you'd lived in this century all along."

"Oh, I don't know about that."

Soon we told Annemarie and Celestia of our plans. They said they'd been invited to stay in another hut nearby. "My parents are staying with Jael," Celestia added.

I gave my daughter a hug. "Sleep tight, Honey," I said. "See you in the morning."

"G'night, Mom."

***

The sleeping arrangements were a little better than the cave. At least here, there was a kind of frame elevating the sleeping mat off the floor of the hut. After all the food and conversation at the Agape Meal, I had no trouble falling asleep.

The first rays of dawn were coming in the cracks around the door, when I opened my eyes. Daiah was stirring something in a pot hung over the cooking fire. "Did you sleep well, Ginna?"

"Like a rock, I think."

"Darien has already gone out to check the perimeter guard-posts. When he gets back, breakfast should be ready."

Whatever she was cooking was beginning to smell delicious. 'I should've eaten more at the Meal,' I thought, making a note of this for next time.

"How often do you have the Agape Meal?"

"Every seventh day. And sometimes we have special worship times for holidays."

"Then we arrived on a good day, didn't we?"

Just as she was about to respond, Darien entered the door, stooping to keep from bumping his head on the lentil. "Mmm! Smells good, Daiah." He kissed her on top of the head.

Soon the three of us were sitting with warm bowls, sipping carefully. It tasted like some kind of cereal grains, crushed, and mixed with fruit, and some kind of milky substance. I'd already learned not to ask too many questions, as long as the food tasted good.

"Where are the children?" Darien asked.

"They went over to practice some of their lessons with Jace."

"Have you seen Annemarie this morning?" he asked, turning to me.

"No. Perhaps they're catching up on their beauty sleep."

"Where did they stay last night?"

"I can't remember the name Celestia gave," I shrugged.

"I think she said they were staying at the Torova's," Daiah said.

Darien nodded but didn't make any comment.

"I think I'll stretch my legs," I said, when my bowl was finished. "My knees don't do well with all this sitting on the floor."

"The sun is warming," Darien said. "But it's still chilly in the shade."

"Thanks for the weather report," I laughed, as I put on the only jacket I had and stooped to go out the door.

All of the snow from the previous day was melted, except for isolated patches in the shadiest spots. Once my eyes adapted to the light, I set off on a walk around the perimeter of the compound. I was about halfway around when Martina joined me.

"How did you sleep, Ginna?"

"You're the second person to ask me that," I laughed. "I slept well. How about you?"

"Oh, fine. How are you getting along here?"

I turned and looked at her, wondering what she was getting at. "Well, if you mean, do I feel at home, I'm not sure. Daiah is easy to talk to, and she's good at making a person feel comfortable."

"You know, I'm told her name means 'Compassion' in some ancient language."

"Well, it certainly fits her," I nodded.

"Have you seen Celestia today?" she asked.

"No, I haven't seen either of them. Do you know where they stayed last night?"

"No. I saw them telling you, though."

"Daiah said it was someplace called Torova's."

"I think that's the hut next to Darien's. Let's go see if they're up yet."

Just as we got to the door of the hut Martina had pointed out, the door opened, and a tall young man stepped out. "Good day, Tomas," said Martina. "Is my daughter out of bed yet?"

Tomas looked very puzzled. "How would I know?"

"Didn't she and Annemarie sleep here?"

"No one was here except my wife and me," he shrugged.

My heart was beginning to pound. "Perhaps I heard the name wrong," I said, looking around and trying not to panic.

Martina stepped back and pulled me with her. "We need to get Darien," she said.

As soon as we reached Darien and Daiah's hut, she was calling out her brother's name. He poked his head out the door, but the smile on his face disappeared when he saw hers. "What's wrong?"

"Celestia and Annemarie didn't stay at Torova's last night."

"What?"

"We need to find where they are," I cried.

"Come with me," he said, pulling both of us along, as he walked quickly toward the low building in the center of the compound.

Soon a bell was ringing, apparently calling an assembly. I could tell by all the puzzled faces this wasn't a common occurrence. Once most of the residents of the compound were assembled, Darien stepped to the podium used as a pulpit the night before.

"Has anyone seen Celestia and the girl who came with her, Annemarie—Ginna's daughter? Does anyone know whose hut they slept in last night?"

There came a lot of murmurs and shaking heads. By now, my heart was pounding so hard in my chest I began to feel faint. Martina was gripping my shoulder tightly. Jon saw us from across the room, and came to his wife's side. Then I felt myself sliding slowly toward the floor. The room spun for a second, and the next thing I knew, Jon was bending over me.

"Here, she's just fainted," his voice said, sounding strangely far away. "She'll be all right."

"What's happened?" I asked, weakly.

"No one knows where they are," I heard Martina say.

"Don't worry. They can't have gone far," another voice said. It sounded like Daiah.

"But my coordinate-chart for Tornatoh is gone." I heard Darien's voice say, from several meters away.

By this time, Jon had lifted me into his arms, carrying me out the door and toward the Infirmary, with Martina holding tightly to my hand.

Blackness came over my eyes again.

The next thing I heard was voices:

"They must have hatched this plot themselves," came Jon's voice.

"You're the one who taught her to cross the GAP." Martina's voice was angry and accusing.

"Well, I didn't think she would be so foolish—to go to one of the largest cities on Earth, practically alone."

"But what can we do?" This sounded like Jael.

"There's nothing we can do right now—except wait," said Jon.

CHAPTER 9

ANOTHER GAP

I knew I'd slept for quite awhile when I opened my eyes. The small patch of sun which was on the floor by my bed had moved all the way across the room. Looking around me, I saw no one in sight until I turned my head to look at the bed next to mine. Immediately, I recognized Irina. Her eyes were looking at me in a puzzled way.

"Somehow, I feel I should know you," she said at last.

'Here we go again with the attempts to explain the unexplainable,' I thought.

"You met her in a sense, Mother." I heard Martina's voice, and realized she was sitting on the other side of Irina's bed. "She was 'within' me when we had our reunion in Celeton."

"My name is Ginna," I said, nodding to her.

"She's visited Jon, Jael, and me a great deal. She 'became' a part of me, in a Time-GAP experiment Jon did many years ago."

Irina's eyes grew wider, but apparently she was accustomed to her daughter being involved with strange undertakings. "I see," she nodded. "And where are you from, Ginna?"

"Actually, I'm from Earth, but in the Twenty-first Century—long before this time."

"Really?"

"Celestia brought Ginna and her daughter, Annemarie, to see us. We'd hoped to help them find Annemarie's father."

"He has to be from this time because I never knew a man in my own time."

Irina's green eyes were gleaming now. "This is a very strange occurrence."

Martina took her mother's hand. "We hadn't intended it to happen, Mother."

"But now, our daughters have disappeared," I said.

"My family seems to have trouble staying together for long," Irina sighed.

"It's better since we've all married," Martina added.

Irina merely closed her eyes then. I could see she was tiring quickly. Martina realized this, also, and gently placed her mother's hand on the bed's blanket. Then she moved to the chair closest to my bed.

I was closing my eyes, too, trying to keep the tears back as I felt Martina take my hand.

"The last thing I remember is Jon saying all we can do is wait."

"That's right," she sighed. "But I'm not sure I can just keep waiting. How are you feeling, Ginna?"

"I feel fine, I think. Let me get up." I pulled myself to the edge of the bed and sat up. When I got onto my feet, I felt a little light-headed, but it soon passed. "Let's see if they'll let me walk down the hall."

Soon, we were walking up and down the corridor in the small infirmary building, with Martina holding my arm to keep me steady.

"We must do something, Martina."

"I know. Our daughters—both being first-born—have a head start on us, though."

"But I did help you cross the GAP back when we met Raina in Colorado."

"I was just thinking about that, Ginna. You're first-born, even though I'm not. If we could just find the coordinates they used."

"I remember hearing Darien say his map for Tornatoh was missing."

Martina was gripping my arm more than necessary now. I put my hand on hers and gently eased it away. "Not so tight."

"Oh, sorry," she almost laughed. "I'm getting too emotional, again. That's always been my weakness. Here, let's sit on this bench."

We settled ourselves on a wooden bench near one of the overhead windows of the building. I could guess why all the windows were above our heads—to keep prying eyes from seeing what was inside. But at least they let in some of the late afternoon light.

"I think I can find some coordinates for Tornatoh," she said, once we could see no one in the hallway. "I can re-trace their search from yesterday. I'm sure they've tried to zero-in on the latest address for Garek in Tornatoh."

"I'll do my best to help with the crossing," I nodded.

"There *is* one more thing I can do, too. "

"What's that?"

"Well, do you remember the first time you met Jon and Jael—what Jon said about the two of them?"

"Sure, Jon said there was some special chemistry between them which enhanced his power. Something to do with a power of the last-born."

"It might not be just the last-born," she said. "I think it's a power of any younger sibling."

"Well, that counts me out," I shrugged.

"But not me," she whispered. "I think I know how it works now. If I can just focus on the images of the *people* we need to find."

Now I was beginning to feel a tingle of hope for the first time in a long while. "So we focus on Celestia and Annemarie."

"And Garek," she added.

"Yes, if they *have* found him that gives us an even better chance of hitting the right place."

"And the right time. Jon will be furious, though," she sighed. "Darien, too."

"Still, Annemarie is all I have in the world—at least in my world—I just can't lose her."

I was beginning to cry again. Martina put her arms around me and just held me.

At last, I felt I could talk again. "So, what do we do first?"

"I'll do a reverse search on the Terminal. You try to get them to let you out of this place sometime tomorrow. Then we can meet—hmm—where should we meet?"

"How about behind Jael's hut?"

"That sounds good. Let's try for sunset tomorrow."

"Okay," I nodded.

"Now, we'd better get you back to your bed. Your job tonight is to get a good rest, so tomorrow you can con-vince them you're ready to be released."

***

I did my best to sleep that night, but it eluded me much of the time. Trying to let my mind rest, I lay with my eyes closed, pretending to sleep. Then I tried using guided imagery—imagining myself floating on a cloud, or in a still pool of water. But desperate thoughts kept intruding, and I couldn't shut them out:

'Will we find the girls? What if something has happened to them? Will we be putting them in more danger by going, or by staying here? And what will it be like to finally see Garek with my own eyes? What will he think of the real me? How will he react to Annemarie?'

It was during one of these attempts at sleep that I heard Martina come in and sit beside Irina's bed. I kept my eyes closed, hoping I wouldn't disturb their time together.

"Mother," I heard Martina whisper softly. "I really need to talk to you."

"What's wrong, dear?"

"Ginna and I are going to cross the GAP and look for our daughters in Tornatoh, but please don't tell anyone."

"You aren't telling Jon or Darien, are you?"

"No. We can't. They'd stop us—and we must go, Mother. I know this in my heart."

"So why are you telling me, Martina?"

"Well, I just want you to know how much I love you, Mother. And I think you're the only one who really understands why we have to do this for our daughters."

There was a long silence, and I could hear both of them breathing.

At last, Irina's voice came quietly. "Yes, I do know. I did whatever I could to find you and Jael. And thanks to the Lord's provisions, I was able to finally be with you again."

Then I heard the sound of Martina embracing her mother. "Thank you, I knew you'd understand. The other reason I wanted to tell you is if we don't make it back in a few days, you can tell them what we did, and why."

"I'll pray every waking moment that all of you will return safely," sighed Irina. "I love you so much, Martina."

Her voice broke, and I could hear both of them quietly crying. Tears were filling my eyes by now, too, as I thought of my own mother, Lauren, gone for many years now. How I wished she was here to give me a comforting hug. I tried to imagine it. And then strangely, I did feel as though someone—or something—was indeed holding me, sending comfort through my tired body. So, at last, I fell asleep.

***

The last rays of the sunset were painting the forest and fields in an orange hue, when Martina and I met behind Jael's hut.

"Did you find what we needed, Martina?"

"Yes, here are the coordinates. I couldn't get the right clothes for us, though."

"What do you mean?"

"Well, people will be able to tell we're Rebels by our ragged, old-style clothing."

"Perhaps it happened to the girls, too."

"That's one thing I'm afraid of."

"What can we do?"

"Well, put on this jacket of Jon's. At least it looks more modern than what you've been wearing. Now, you need to concentrate on those coordinates, while I focus on the girls and Garek."

"I heard you telling Irina last night."

"I wondered if you were really asleep," she smiled.

"Did you say anything to Jael?"

"No. I really want to, but it's just too risky. This way, no one here will be in danger—hopefully."

"Unless what the girls did has caused trouble already," I added.

"All the more reason we need to go now, Ginna."

"Okay, I'm as ready as I'll ever be." I took the coordinates she'd put on a reading-chip for me and tried to focus all my energy and mind on them, closing my eyes.

I could hear Martina softly repeating the names, "Annemarie, Celestia, and Garek."

Suddenly the ground beneath me seemed to tilt. I reached out and grabbed Martina's arm, and she responded by holding mine tightly, too. Then my feet felt as though they were floating in air. There was a sound like wind rushing in my ears.

Then the air seemed to vibrate with a new sound. It was like drums beating and horns blaring. Opening my eyes, I found we were standing along a city street. There *were* drums and horns—in a band marching by, down the center of the street.

People all around us were cheering and waving flags. Colors of black and green seemed to be the most dominant ones in the banners and decorations around us.

"What is this?" I managed to get Martina to hear me over the noise.

"Some kind of celebration," she shouted back.

"I can see that. But what for?"

She answered by pulling me back from the edge of the street and toward a narrow alley between two brick buildings.

"I think it's International Day," she said, when we'd reached a place where the din was less.

"What's that?"

"Well, in my time here on Earth, all the nations have merged into one International Union. This must be the day of its celebration—like your old-time Independence Day."

"Oh yeah, Fourth of July. But are we in the right place? Is this Tornatoh?"

"Should be," she shrugged. "It's one of the International Capitals, but it seems we've time-shifted a bit. It's morning here, and it was evening when we left the compound."

"Maybe that's why we didn't find the girls? Didn't you concentrate on them enough?"

She shook her head. "I don't know. This is the first

time I've tried to do it. Maybe I need to focus on just one person."

"So how can we know for sure where we are?"

"If we can find the Temple of the Way—"

"Oh, that's right," I nodded. "I remember. Is it still standing in this time?"

"It was the last time I was here, which was only a few years ago," she said.

With no idea what direction to go first, we set off for an area where the crowds were thinner. At least we could push our way through, once we were away from the parade route.

There seemed to be thousands of people milling up and down the streets of the city. Many were stopping at small food or beverage stalls set up on the sidewalks. The food being sold didn't look familiar to me, but some of the smells were tantalizing.

"Hope you're not hungry," said Martina. "I don't have a way to buy any of this stuff. We can't get credits anymore."

I only nodded, as the grim reality of what the ostracized Believers faced became even clearer to me.

We were climbing up a gently sloping street now.

"This looks vaguely familiar," I said.

"To me, too. I'm wondering if it's High Street."

"You mean the place where that old man had his shop?"

"You do remember, don't you?"

I nodded again. It was very strange, but I did seem to be able to recognize things I'd seen all those years ago when I'd been 'inside' Martina and we'd come with Jon and Jael and Soren and Dom to look for the Temple of the Way.

Soon we were at the crest of the hill, and there on our right was a small shop with incredibly dusty windows. It looked like it had been abandoned for many years.

"Doesn't look like anyone is here," I sighed.

Martina merely nodded, but tried the door's handle anyway. To our surprise, it moved, and the door creaked open.

"Same rusty hinge?" I half-smiled.

Again, she only nodded.

The light was dim inside the shop, and the shelves along both walls were empty. This didn't look promising. I found myself breathing carefully to keep from getting a nose-full of dust.

"Anybody here?" Martina called tentatively.

At first there was no sound, but then there came a slight shuffling.

"Probably just a rat," I whispered, trying not to shudder.

Suddenly, we heard a loud *thump*. Dust motes flew all around us, catching the bits of sunlight managing to find their way through the filthy windows.

"I have no credits," came a raspy-sounding voice. "Go away!"

"We don't want credits, just information," Martina called.

"None of that here, either," the voice rasped again.

"Please sir, do you remember how we came to get 'invitations' to the temple fountains, many years ago?"

"Who are you? Your voice sounds familiar, and I never forget a voice. Were you the ones with that strange winged cat?"

"Yes, the feier-cat!" Martina called. "And we were the ones who came back. You told us how to find the True Fountain in the great eastern desert."

Suddenly a figure appeared, looming up into the swirls of dust in front of us. He was very bent, and looked so ancient I almost thought he was a mummy, not alive at all.

"I *do* remember you," the old voice croaked again, and the figure pointed a bony finger at Martina. "But not you," he added, turning to me.

"She was 'inside' me then," Martina said.

"Looks too old to be your daughter, but perhaps…" he grumbled.

I tried not to giggle. He thought Martina meant she was pregnant with me—and then I hoped this explanation would work, because I doubted there was any other way we could explain the true story to him.

"Well, come on," he growled suddenly as he turned and led us through a side door to our right. Perhaps this was where he'd appeared from so suddenly.

"Sir, we're Believers," I whispered. "Like you." I'm not sure what made me say this. The words just seemed to come out of my mouth.

Martina was almost shooting daggers at me with her eyes, but the old man looked up at me and cracked a toothless smile.

"I thought so," he whispered back. "I could tell all those years ago when you first came to my shop."

"How could you tell then?" Martina asked. "We weren't even sure what we believed ourselves."

"Some of you were questioning," he nodded. "But you were asking the right kind of questions, the honest ones. Now-a-days people don't ask questions, but they should."

By this time, we were in a small room with a rickety table and chairs. "Please sit," he nodded toward two of the chairs. "I'm too old to talk standing up anymore."

Once we were seated, he gave a deep sigh. "I'm sorry I have no refreshment to offer you lovely ladies."

Martina just smiled at him. "Please don't worry about it. Believe me, I understand how things are in these times."

Now I knew for sure that he was a Believer, too. "How do you get any food for yourself?" I asked.

"I have dear friends who risk their lives to bring me what they can. How do you manage in this city, my dears?"

"We aren't from here," Martina said quickly. "We're trying to live off the land in the wilds."

"Why did you come to this dangerous place then?"

"We're searching for our daughters," I murmured.

He looked closely at me, but didn't say any more.

"We're not sure where to look next," Martina added. "We think they came here searching for a man named Garek."

"I know several men with that name," he shrugged. "It was a common name a few decades back."

Silence settled over us again. I felt my heart sinking. How were we ever going to find Annemarie and Celestia in this huge strange city?

"Sir, is the Temple of the Way still standing?" Martina asked, when the silence became more than we could bear.

He nodded slowly, but then he changed to shaking his head. "The building still stands and the fountains still spout to music," he sighed. "But now it is called 'The Temple of Union'—the idea of there being one 'Way' to find God is taboo in the International Union—and in this city."

I could hear deep sadness in his voice, and found myself reaching to take his hand.

He looked at me in surprise when he felt my touch. Then his lips formed a small smile. "Tell me about who you are seeking and what you believe, my dears."

"My daughter came seeking a man named Garek

Carson, because she believes he is her father," I sighed. "I'm not sure how to explain what *I believe*. But I do have faith in God—and his son, Kristos, who was born here on Earth long ago."

"Praise be his name," he whispered.

Martina moved closer to him and took his other hand. "We crossed the GAP to get here," she said softly. "But something went wrong, and we didn't find the place where our daughters were. I'm not sure what we can do next. Yes, we are Believers—all my family is. We came here from Terres because we hoped we'd find the True King reigning here."

"He was Lord and King for many long years—in all true hearts," the old man sighed. "But now we're approaching the end, when the Evil One has been released for a time. I pray the Final Battle will come soon, for there are so few left now who believe or remember the King of Heaven and Earth."

"Sometimes I'm not sure we can survive long enough to see the last days," said Martina.

"Whether we live on—or die before he comes—we will be with him in Heaven, regardless," he nodded to both of us.

"Do you think we should try looking at the Temple?" I asked.

"There's no point. They've strayed too far," he sighed. "What was that name you gave? Carson?"

"Yes!" My heart started to race. "Do you know him?"

"I've heard one of my friends mention the name." He nodded his head slowly toward me. "Let me think."

"We have an address for him that my daughter found on a Netsearch, Promontory Road." Martina sounded excited now.

The old man was sitting very still with his eyes closed. I began to wonder if he'd fallen asleep, the way elderly people do sometimes. When I reached up to his shoulder to try gently shaking it, Martina shook her head at me. Then suddenly he opened his eyes. "Patience, my dears," he said sharply. "My mind doesn't work as quickly as it used to."

We both looked down and tried to keep from commenting. Anything we said now would just interrupt his train of thought.

"I do have a friend who lives near Promontory Road," he said at last. "He was here a few days ago to bring me some food. He calls himself Elias."

"Did he ever wander in the eastern desert?" Martina asked. "We met an old man out there who said his name was Eli."

"I don't think so," he shrugged. "But he did mention a neighbor of his named Carson. Perhaps it was the same man, since Elias does live near the road you seek."

"Can you please tell us how to get to this road?" I knew my voice was beginning to sound like begging.

Suddenly he smiled. "I can do better. Elias gave me

the coordinates for his home, just in case I was in desperate need."

"Will you come with us?" Martina asked.

"Oh, no. I will be too much of a burden in your search. My calling is to stay in this little place on High Street."

"That reminds me of something Eli said," I added.

"Yes, he said his calling was to help searchers in the desert. By the way, we don't even know *your* name," said Martina.

"Most of my friends call me Kai," he said softly. "But my full name is Malakai."

"There's a prophet in The Book called Malachi," I said excitedly. "Are you a prophet, too?"

"All I know is I'm here to help seekers find the true way to the Lord."

"Well, this is the second time in our lives you've helped *us*," said Martina.

I was nodding, too.

"You must go now," he said suddenly. "The parades will be over soon, and people like you will be too obvious again. Here are the coordinates." He pulled a tiny thumb-chip from his pocket.

Martina seemed to know how to read it, and told me the coordinates I needed to cross us to this new place.

"What will you do, if you give us these?" I asked. "Won't you need them in an emergency?"

"No," he smiled. "I will not flee to Elias when my time comes. When they come for me—not 'if'—I will be happy to be going to be with my Lord at last."

The light in his eyes suddenly grew, and I felt a sort of envy for him and his certainty in his faith. I wanted to be this way, but knew I still had too many doubts and fears.

"How can we thank you enough?" Martina was saying.

"I just pray you will find your loved ones, my dears. By the way, what are *your* names?"

"I'm Ginna, and this is Martina."

He stood slowly then, and I could tell it was painful for him. "I'll be glad to trade in this old body for a heavenly one," he smiled. "Now, off with you. And may Kristos bless you and yours."

Martina grabbed my hands, and I closed my eyes, trying to concentrate on the coordinates she'd given me. I could hear her voice repeating the name 'Garek', as the room seemed to spin away from us, and my feet felt as though they'd left the ground.

CHAPTER 10

MORE TWISTS AND TURNS

Once again, the ground seemed to rise up to meet my feet. The only sounds I heard were the slight hum of wheeled vehicles moving on pavement nearby. Quickly, I opened my eyes and saw we were indeed beside a narrower road than we'd been on before.

In front of us was a low, buff-colored house. The windows were curtained, so we couldn't see inside. Just as I was about to turn to Martina, the front door opened and a man in strange clothing stepped out. He had on skin-tight black leggings, and his tunic had large epaulettes that stuck out a good ten centimeters past his shoulders. It was a strange color, too, a very bright vermillion.

He took one look at us and grimaced. Then he strode quickly toward us and grabbed our hands with each of his.

"Come!" his high-pitched voice said sharply. "You must get indoors dressed like that."

Before we could say a word, he literally dragged us through his front door, locking it behind us.

"What's going on here?" Martina demanded.

"Where is Kai?" was the only reply the man made.

"Are you Elias?" I asked tentatively.

Then his manner seemed to soften. "Kai sent you?"

"Yes, sir," said Martina.

"Is he well?"

"As well as such an old man can be," I shrugged.

"He gave us the coordinates you'd given him," Martina added.

Elias shook his head at this. "That foolish, dear old man."

"What?" I asked.

"He's given them away again."

"You mean the coordinates?"

"This is the second time he's done it. Your story must have touched him." He'd seated himself on a bright purple chair by this time, and now motioned for us to sit on a low cushion of the same garish color, across from him. "You'd best tell me your story now, too."

"We are Believers," I began.

"I could tell that by your clothing. Tell me something I don't already know."

The clipped sound of his voice was beginning to annoy me. Did he want to listen to us, or not? I let out an inadvertent sigh. Then Martina spoke up:

"We live in the wilds, not the city. And we believe our daughters have come to this part of the city, searching for a man named Garek Carson."

"Yes, I've heard the name. There's a person over the crest of the hill behind my house who has that name."

"My daughter believes he's her father," I added.

He raised his eyebrows at this. "Carson is not a Believer."

Now it was Martina's turn to sigh. "I did try to talk to him about faith many times."

"Well the end hasn't come yet, so it's still not too late," said Elias. " 'Even now the fields are white for harvest,' as Kristos told his followers."

" 'Pray the Lord of the harvest to send workers into his fields'," I heard my voice say.

Suddenly the man smiled at me, and the clouds of doubt in his eyes disappeared. "So, you truly are Believers."

We nodded silently.

"Non-believers don't know how to quote The Book," he said then. "Now, tell me, how did you ever find Kai?"

"I recognized his shop from when I was here over twenty years ago," said Martina.

Now his face registered even more surprise. "Indeed?"

"My name is Martina, and this is Ginna. We each have daughters who are about twenty-five Standard Years old. We believe they crossed the GAP to come here. They would have been wearing clothing similar to ours. My daughter, Celestia, has long dark hair like mine."

"They're about the same build and height," I added. "Except that Celestia's eyes are deep brown. My daughter, Annemarie, is taller than I am, and has wavy blonde hair. Her eyes are a brilliant blue, not brown like mine. She is much prettier than I am. My hair is just this mousey brown."

"Don't belittle yourself," he smiled at me. "You have an inner beauty that few women I've met display."

I felt myself beginning to blush and looked down. "Have you seen anyone meeting their descriptions recently?"

He shook his head. "I seldom go outdoors, Ginna— only when I must—and then I take great care to blend into the populace around here, hence my outlandish-looking outfit."

Suddenly, I found it strange that a person had to dress in such a gaudy and noticeable style to 'fit in'.

Then he went on. "I have a question for you now, I can tell by your manner you've never met this man Carson. So how can he be your daughter's father?"

I took a frightened glance at Martina. We hadn't thought of how to answer a question like this.

"I—umm—adopted Annemarie." I said the first plausible thing coming to mind and heard Martina sigh in relief.

"Yes, that's correct. However, *I* once met Garek, over

twenty years ago in Salien. We were both working on a Forestry Commission project."

Elias sat quietly for a long time after we spoke. Finally, he took my hand in his and sighed.

"The only thing I can do for you is tell you how to get to his house," he said at last. "I've not seen him for several days, and have seen no one matching your descriptions of your daughters."

He rose from the chair quickly then. Stepping to a closet near the front door, he began pulling out jackets and leggings similar to the ones he was wearing.

"I don't know if these will be the right size, but they will have to do."

"We don't want to take your clothing," I said.

"Nonsense! These are here for anyone in need. I need only one outfit for myself."

"Well, if you're sure," Martina said.

Meanwhile, he'd pulled two tunics and pairs of pants from the growing pile he was making on the floor. "Try these on," he said, motioning us toward a door to his left.

Once we were in the adjacent room, and the door was closed, I turned to Martina. "Do you think we can trust this guy?"

"I don't see any other choice now," she sighed.

I shrugged and began changing into the strange colorful clothes. Soon we were looking at each other and trying not to giggle.

"I'm not sure chartreuse is your color, Martina."

"Well, that shade of lavender makes you look pale. Maybe we should switch?"

We traded tunics, and fortunately the fits were similar. "I'm glad he didn't give us one in the color *he* was wearing," she said, as we looked at each other again.

"That's for sure," I chuckled. As I did so, I noticed Jon's jacket lying beside me on the floor. "I don't want to leave Jon's jacket here. He'll need it."

Martina picked it up and quickly folded it. The she lifted her tunic and tied the sleeves of the jacket around her waist. When she pulled the tunic down, it didn't show much. "How does that look?"

"Fine to me. Does it feel awkward?"

"No. I often do this, since we dress in layers to be prepared for any sudden weather changes in the wilds."

Then we opened the door and stepped out into the central room again. Elias looked at us and smiled. "I think that will do," he nodded.

"Sir, I want to ask one more question," said Martina. "Have you ever guided people to the Fountain in the Desert?"

His eyes showed great surprise at this. "Not I, but my father did for many years."

"Was he called 'Eli'?"

He nodded. "You met him?"

Now it was our turn to nod. "Yes, but it was over twenty years ago."

Suddenly I saw tears glistening in his eyes. "Is he gone now?" I whispered.

"I'll meet him again at the gates."

"I'm so sorry," Martina said.

"Oh, don't be sad for him," said Elias in a stronger voice. "He's in the best place, and before too long, we'll all be joining him."

I found myself nodding again. "But I hope we can find Celestia and Annemarie first."

"Then you must go now," he sighed. "It will be safer in this area if you walk. Promontory Road is the first cross-road you come to when you head east up my street, Crescent Lane."

Now we understood the need for these bright clothes. We were going to walk openly up the streets, trying to hide in plain sight.

"Sir, how can we ever thank you?"

"There is no need, Ginna," he smiled. "Each of us merely does what he can. 'May the Lord watch between me and thee'," his high-pitched voice added.

" 'While we are absent one from the other'," I finished for him.

He smiled and nodded. " 'May the words of my mouth, and the meditations of my heart be acceptable in thy sight'."

" 'Oh Lord, my strength and my redeemer',” I added.

Then we all moved toward the door he'd pulled us through, such a short time ago. There was nothing left to say, so we stepped out into the bright light of afternoon. Quickly and quietly, the door closed behind us, leaving Martina and me alone on the now-silent street.

As we started uphill on Crescent Lane, I suddenly realized we had no idea which way to turn when we reached the junction with Promontory Road. My heart began to pound, and I couldn't help but wonder if the man was setting us up. Was it true, as he'd said, that only Believers quoted The Book in these days? Or was he a very clever spy for the authorities?

Just as we reached the crest of the hill, however, we saw there was only one direction to take for Promontory Road, as it joined this street in a 'T'. I sighed with relief.

Martina didn't seem to have these doubts, for she just kept walking briskly, looking at the numbers on the houses.

"What number are we looking for, Martina?"

"Twenty-seven hundred."

Just as she spoke, I noticed a house on our right with the front door swinging open in the wind. This didn't look normal. And at the same moment, I noticed the house number: *2700*. "There it is!" I cried, and began running toward it.

She was right behind me, as we burst through the door, into a room which looked like it was recently ransacked. My heart seemed to sink all the way down to my shoes.

"What's happened?" I moaned.

"I would say the authorities were here."

"Did they arrest him—or them?"

"There's no way to tell," she sighed.

I reached down and picked up a scrap of paper from the floor. It was the only one in sight—everything else was electronic equipment, and pieces of furnishings. "Look!"

"Is that paper?"

"Yes, but what does it mean?" I asked.

"Paper is extremely rare in this time," she said excitedly.

I shook my head. Of course! To me it was commonplace to find scraps of paper, but in this time, books were very rare.

"Is there any writing on it?"

I handed it to her, and she turned it over, carefully examining both sides, and then shook her head.

"Garek used to write me letters," she was saying. "This *must* be his place."

As quietly as we could, we explored the rest of the house, but there were just more signs of the authorities' search and destruction. We didn't find any more scraps of paper, but we did find a scrap of cloth that made Martina cringe.

"This was the color of Celestia's tunic," she gasped.

"Does this mean they've been captured?"

She nodded silently. As she did this, I noticed a cup of tea sitting on the floor beside a chair. Somehow it hadn't been spilled. I dipped a finger carefully into it, but it was cold. "No one has been her for awhile," I sighed.

Martina sniffed at the tea when I showed her the cup. "That smells like chamomile—a fairly common tea in the wilds—another sign the girls were probably here."

"What can we do now, Martina?"

"Last time I just concentrated on Garek," she said at last. "And we did get close to his house."

"But we also had coordinates for Elias."

"I know."

"We have no idea where they've been taken."

"I'm going to concentrate every ounce of my being on Celestia," she said grimly. "You need to just focus on crossing a GAP."

"Any GAP? How do I do that?"

"I don't know!" I knew the snap in her voice was anxiety, and not anger at me, so I tried to ignore it.

"Okay, I'll do the best I can," I sighed, taking her hands.

***

The next thing I knew, we were in a dimly-lit room, and everything looked gray. Rubbing my eyes, I began to make out shadows seated on the floor beside a wall. Above them was a small square window with bars on it. The light coming in seemed to be very dim, compared to what we'd seen on Promontory Road.

"Mom? Is that really you?" My daughter's voice sounded frightened and hopeful, at the same time.

"Annemarie?"

There was no answer, except hands suddenly gripping mine, pulling me toward her. "How did you find us?"

My head still felt like it was spinning, and I tried to get my eyes to focus on her face. "Is that you, Annemarie?"

"Yes, Mom, it's really me. Is that Martina with you?"

I turned then, and saw Martina step closer, kneeling beside her own daughter's still form, lying on the floor. She shook her gently, and to my relief, Celestia sat up rubbing her eyes.

As our eyes grew more accustomed to the dim light, we could see that the four of us were in what appeared to be a small prison cell.

"How did you get here?" Celestia asked.

"Ginna crossed the GAP, and I assisted by focusing on you."

"I don't understand what all that means, so I'll just take your word for it," said Annemarie.

"How did you get put in this prison?" I asked.

"Someone spotted that we were dressed like Rebels," sighed Celestia.

Martina nodded to me, but neither of us spoke. It was a moot point now. In fact, now that we were in prison, too, it didn't matter what we were wearing either.

"I don't suppose anyone has any ideas about getting out of here," Annemarie said.

"Well, we 'crossed' in, so perhaps we can 'cross' out, too," said Martina.

"Annemarie and I tried, but we couldn't do it."

"Perhaps it's the thick stone walls," I suggested.

"There's another problem," said a deep male voice just then. "There are GAP-guards."

Our daughters didn't seem surprised, but Martina and I nearly went into shock. Then a third figure, curled in the corner of the cell, sat up and looked intently at us.

"This time I know it's Martina," he said. "You and your daughter look very much alike, except for your eyes." I thought I could hear a slight chuckle in his voice, and I knew who he was before anyone spoke another word.

"Garek!" Martina gasped. "What are you doing here?"

"Oh, just arrested for harboring Rebels."

"He got caught trying to help us, Mom," said Celestia.

Now Garek stood, and I saw him with my own eyes at last. He was a tall and muscular man with graying hair. His blue eyes shone as he looked at the four of us. "Okay, who is this other newcomer?"

"Uh, this is *my* mother—Ginna," said Annemarie.

He stepped forward to see me better, and I could

sense him getting puzzled. "I've met Annemarie, and I see how much she resembles my daughter, Jelaine. Have I met you before, Ginna?"

'Here goes,' I thought. "I think you have, in a way."

"Well, so far today I've been visited by the daughter of my former lover—Celestia, the one who I know isn't *my* daughter. And then I met a young woman I never knew existed who looks like me—"

"And now you're seeing Annemarie's mother," I said.

"But I've never seen you before. I'm sure I would remember you, if I'd—uh, been intimate enough to father a child."

"Well, the last time you saw me, I was living 'within' Martina. So, you wouldn't *see* me, but you may have *sensed* me."

"This is sounding really weird, I must admit."

"That's exactly how I felt, when Jon and Martina took me back to my own time, and I found myself pregnant."

"But how can you prove it was me who did this to you?"

"All I can tell you is I slept with no man in my own time, and only two here—while I was 'in' Martina."

"And the other one was the brown-eyed Jon," he sighed. "But Annemarie has blue eyes."

"Yes."

"So, what do you want from me, child support?"

"No. We've managed just fine so far, my daughter and I."

"It was more Celestia and me, Garek," Martina spoke at last. "I felt you should know about this other daughter of yours." Martina had a look of determination in her eyes that I'd seen before.

"I see." He stepped closer to me. "And your name is Ginna?"

I nodded, but found I'd lost my voice.

With a strong, yet gentle touch I somehow remembered well, he took my hands in his. For a few moments he just looked into my eyes, and then he pulled me closer into his warm embrace.

"There *is* something familiar about this," he said quietly. "Perhaps there's some truth in your story."

"Why would we put ourselves in this kind of danger for a lie?" said Martina.

"You have a point there," he chuckled. "But what do we do now?"

"I think we should try crossing the GAP to get out of here," said Celestia. "Perhaps with three first-born, we can do it."

"And Martina has some power to focus on getting to specific people," I added.

"But what about me?" Garek asked. "Do I come with you to join the Rebels, or stay behind in this cell?" He'd released me from his embrace, and I felt my head beginning to spin with anxiety.

"I guess that's your choice," Annemarie sighed. "But I

wish you *would* come—if just to get to know me." I could hear the wistful sound of her voice, and realized how not having a father all those years had taken a greater toll on her than I thought.

"Well, I always thought of myself as your basic law-abiding citizen, until you girls showed up."

"I'm sorry," murmured Celestia. "It's my fault for bringing us here."

"No, I wanted to come even more than you," my daughter said.

"There will be no safety for me here, I'm afraid, even if I ever get out of this prison. And I do remember Martina trying to tell me about this Lord you worship."

I saw Martina stand a little taller, as she moved to touch him on the shoulder. "I did that because I really cared about you, Garek."

"Was it just *you* who cared, or Ginna too?"

"I've wondered that for a long time myself," I sighed.

"Well, I can't say how any of this will end, but I think I prefer life as a Rebel to life in this cell."

"Then you *will* come?" asked Annemarie.

"Might as well," he shrugged.

"All right then," said Martina. "All of us need to join hands in a circle. Don't let anything break your grips. Ginna and Celestia know what to do to cross the GAP. I'll focus on Jon. Hopefully that will get us back to a time close to when we left."

"Which was my original plan, Mom," said Celestia. "In fact, I was going to try to get back to a time just before we left, so no one would even know we'd been gone."

"My, you were ambitious, weren't you?" I said.

"I'm so glad you came for us, Mom," said Annemarie.

Martina formed us into a tight circle by this time. "Okay, enough of this. Everyone close your eyes and focus on the coordinates of Darien's compound."

Again, the floor seemed to melt out from under me. This time the wind was much stronger, trying to pull us apart. My hair felt as though it was being whipped by a hurricane. I could feel Garek's hand tightly gripping my right hand, and Annemarie clinging to my left. I prayed our circle wouldn't break under the strain of the winds. It seemed something was clawing at me, but then suddenly, it was gone.

All around, I could hear sounds of wind rustling the tall grasses of the prairie. Then I made out the sound of wind hissing through the tall evergreens around the compound. Opening my eyes, I saw Jael and Jon running toward us. We were just outside the Infirmary, near the edge of the stockade wall. Then everything went black. I must have fainted again.

CHAPTER 11

HOW TO BE LIGHT

The next thing I saw was a bright light in my eyes. As I tried to open them, pain stabbed across my forehead. Covering my eyes with my hand, I moaned.

"Mom?" came my daughter's near-panicked voice. "What's wrong?"

"Just a headache," I tried to reassure her. "Where am I?"

"In the Infirmary."

"Again? I sure seem to be a wimp lately, always fainting."

"Don't worry," said another voice. "It's just you aren't used to crossing the GAP."

"Is that you, Martina?" I asked, still keeping my sensitive eyes closed.

"Yes, I'm here. Just came by to see how you were."

"That last crossing felt like something was trying to stop us," I sighed.

"Yes, I know. I felt it too, Mom."

"Garek was right. They had some kind of guardian forces on the prison," said Martina. "We couldn't have managed it without at least four first-born. Luckily, Garek is one, too."

"So, his being with us made it possible to escape?"

"Yes, we're fortunate he was willing to help us, Ginna."

My eyes finally were adjusted to the idea of light again, so I opened them carefully. Now I could see Annemarie sitting in the chair close to my bed, holding my hand. Somehow, I hadn't felt this before, but now I tried to squeeze her hand reassuringly. Martina was standing at the foot of my bed.

I found myself compelled to ask my next question, "Where is Garek now?"

"He's at Daiah and Darien's hut," Martina said. "Didn't seem a good idea to put him in Jael's place, with Jon and I."

"Is Jon angry?"

"Not anymore," said my daughter. "Now that we're all safe."

"How long were we gone?"

"About two days in this present time," said Martina. "Mother had just told Jael of our plans, when we showed up."

"What does Garek think of all this?" I asked, finding my mind going back to him persistently.

"He isn't saying much," said Annemarie. "But he's glad he could help us escape the prison—I do know that." There was just a hint of a smile in her voice. I took this to mean she was grateful her supposed-father was glad to help *her*, at least.

"Jon seems to have finally forgiven me, and Garek," Martina whispered then. "All three of us have agreed to leave the past in the past."

"Well, that's good." I closed my eyes again, as my head began to throb harder. 'I wonder if I should have left the past behind, too,' I couldn't help thinking to myself.

"Mom, you should rest. We'll come back when they bring your next meal."

There were other questions I wanted to ask about Garek, but found I hadn't the strength just then. In fact, I dozed off before my daughter even left my side.

***

The next sound I heard was the clatter of a food tray, and someone telling me it was time to eat something. Gingerly I sat up, letting the attendant help me. I was surprised at how weak I still felt. After I ate some of the hot soup on my tray, though, I began to feel more normal. I'd just finished it when Annemarie came in.

"Hi, Mom, you look much better this evening."

"I feel better, too. What day is it?"

"I think it's the day after we got back."

"Have I been sleeping that long?"

"Yes. You must have really needed it," she smiled. "I've gotten permission to take you to the Gathering tonight, though."

I smiled back at her. This was indeed good news—I was glad Annemarie wanted to go to these Gatherings now. Perhaps she was coming back to the Lord she'd been running from too long. Besides, any scene outside of this Infirmary sounded wonderful, and I knew I was also hoping to see Garek, wondering why he hadn't visited me here. "So, when do we go to the Gathering?"

"As soon as you get dressed, Mom."

She helped me get into some clothes she'd brought. I was thankful I didn't have to put on the garish chartreuse tunic I'd been wearing when we returned.

Slowly, I managed to get to my feet. I desperately wanted to walk on my own power, but knew I needed her help—at least at first.

Soon, we were outside in a clear, starry night. The large moon of Earth was full, and shining bright light across the compound. Ahead of us, I could see the candlelight seeping from the high windows of the central building.

When we came through the door, the whispers grew louder. As we sat down, Martina and Jon moved over to join us. In spite of myself, I glanced around, trying to see where Garek was. Finally, I saw him seated between Daiah and Darien, a few rows behind us. 'At least he's here in the Gathering,' I sighed to myself. 'I hope he'll listen and begin to believe.'

Shortly after we arrived, the same gray-haired man who spoke at the first Gathering rose and moved to the center of the room.

"Tonight's reading is from *First Peter, chapter two, verse nine*," he said softly. " 'But you are a chosen people, a holy nation, a people belonging to God, that you may declare the praises of him who called you out of darkness into his wonderful light.' Thank you, True Lord of the Universe, that you have cared enough to reach out and call us."

"Amen!" came several voices.

"We praise you that you still seek those who are lost," said Daiah.

"We're thankful you don't give up on us, your often-wayward children." This was Martina's voice beside me. Then I saw Jon take her hand and rub it reassuringly, in a way I'd felt before, long ago, when I was 'in' her.

Darien's voice was speaking by this time. "Help us to be a light that shines for the world to see, O Lord. Help us to dispel the darkness of the Powers and the System."

"Amen!" said many voices.

"May we be like a city on a hill," said another voice. "Like a beacon that shows the way," someone else added.

"Forgive us for our fears, when we hide our light," came another voice.

I desperately wanted to turn and see Garek's face, wondering what he was thinking of all this. But with them sitting behind us, it would have been too obvious.

Instead, I sat quietly, wiping a few tears from my eyes. 'Why do I feel guilty?' I asked the Lord—and myself. 'I wasn't the one who had the affair—it was Martina. Still, I was there, too. Oh, Lord if I did anything wrong, please forgive me. And, Lord, I'll leave it up to you—whatever is meant to happen now.'

With this, I felt better, like someone had lifted a weight off my shoulders. Suddenly I realized my headache was gone, too. Voices began singing, and soon Annemarie and I joined in:

> *"The King shall come when morning dawns,*
> *and light triumphant breaks,*
> *When beauty gilds the eastern hills, and life to joy awakes.*

> *"Not as of old a little child, to bear and fight and die,*
> *But crowned with glory like the sun, that lights the morning sky.*

> *"The King shall come when morning dawns,*
> *and light and beauty brings.*
> *Hail, to the Lord, thy people pray: Come quickly, King of Kings!"*

I was gripping Annemarie's hand tightly by the end of the song. "That's always been a favorite of mine," I whispered.

"Me too, Mom. Isn't it amazing how some of the songs we knew have been preserved all these centuries?"

I squeezed her hand in agreement. "A good hymn speaks to God's people in any age, Honey."

She nodded.

"Oh, Lord, we pray you will show yourself strong and mighty on behalf of us, your people, small remnant though we are," said the man at the center podium. "May we stay true to you in any tribulation. Amen."

After another silence, people gradually began to rise from their seats and make their way to the tables where the Agape Meal was spread. I moved toward Daiah, and Garek standing shyly behind her.

"Welcome to the Feast," I said to him, nodding, and trying to smile. I felt fear in my gut, wondering if he thought this was all some crazy myth, but he seemed glad to see me and smiled. "Are you feeling better, Ginna?"

"Yes," I nodded, noticing a slight smile on his lips. "I think they'll let me out of that place soon."

"The Infirmary?"

"Yes. Didn't you know where I was?"

"No one told me much," he shrugged.

Well, perhaps this explained his absence. I began to

realize Darien probably felt it best if I recovered first before I was faced with Garek.

"They mean well here," I said.

"Darien seems like a very capable leader," he nodded.

"Are you hungry?" I decided to change the subject.

"Famished! How does this 'Love Feast' work?"

"I see Daiah has at least told you the name," I smiled. "We're supposed to get food for each other, not for ourselves."

He stopped his hand just then, as he was reaching for a piece of fruit. Then he picked it up anyway and offered it to me. I took it, nodding my thanks, and handed a piece of bread to him. "May the Lord be with you," I whispered.

"And with you, too, Ginna."

The room was beginning to spin a little, and I grabbed his arm. "Sorry, I'm just feeling faint again," I murmured.

Quickly, he guided me to a bench and sat us both down. I munched on the fruit, while he ate his bread. Then he rose and got me some of the juice to drink.

"Thank you, Garek."

We ate and drank in silence for a few minutes. I desperately wanted to say something, but couldn't think of how to start.

Finally, he seemed to find words, "I don't quite know what to say to you, Ginna. This is a very unusual circumstance we find ourselves in."

"That's for sure," I nodded. "It's not every day you meet a stranger who happens to be the mother of your daughter."

"The only other case I could think of would be if you'd been artificially inseminated with my sperm." I could hear a slight chuckle in his voice.

"Hmm, I hadn't even thought of that, Garek."

"Well it's probably more common in my time than in yours."

"You know, even though I'm a stranger to you, I have to admit I feel some attraction to you." There—I'd said it aloud, at last.

"You do?"

I found my voice was gone now and only nodded.

"Well, between you and all this religious stuff, I have to admit I'm feeling sort of like a fish out of water here. I'd like to learn more about this Lord, though."

"I feel strange here, too," I said, finding my voice. "After all, this isn't my time—I'm from the early Twenty-first Century—but I am a Believer, as they call themselves here."

His food was gone by now, and he suddenly took my hand in his. Again, I felt a familiar sensation—like I'd known him for a long time.

"It's odd," he whispered. "When I touch you, I do feel as though I've done it before—in some other life."

"That's how it feels to me, too."

We sat for several minutes in silence, just holding hands.

"I think we should just wait and see where this goes—if it even goes anywhere at all," he said finally.

"I agree. We have all the time in the world."

He laughed aloud.

CHAPTER 12

FATHERS AND DAUGHTERS

Annemarie lay on her back in the tall grass, looking up at a blue sky. A few white clouds were drifting overhead. 'When I was a little girl, I would try to find shapes in the clouds,' she thought. 'But I don't seem to have the imagination for it right now.' She closed her eyes, and sighed. The sunlight felt warm and comforting on her face.

"Eh-hmm," said a male voice nearby.

Sitting up quickly, she saw Garek walking toward her. "Am I disturbing something?"

"No, I'm just enjoying the warmth of the sun." She motioned with her hand to the grassy ground beside her. "You're welcome to join me, if you want."

"Thanks." He sat down and pulled his knees up, putting his arms around them.

After a few minutes of silence, he turned toward her. "I feel like I need to get to know you better," he said hesitantly. "I'm finally ready to admit I believe you're my daughter, somehow."

"Mom told me what you said about the sperm bank thing. I guess that's the closest comparison we've come up with, so far."

"Yeah, I guess so."

"And, as far as I'm concerned, you could just leave it at that. I don't want you to feel obligated to care about me."

"Oh, but I do, Annemarie."

She turned and looked into his eyes. "Really?"

He nodded silently.

"Are you sorry you chose to come here with us?" She didn't know where this thought came from. Perhaps she'd seen it his eyes.

"Part of me is, I'll admit. There's a good possibility that if I tried to go back, I'd be arrested as a Rebel, even though I'm not. I probably won't ever see my daughter or my son again."

She heard the pain in his voice, and reached for his arm. "Oh, my gosh! So, my trying to find you has ruined your life."

"Hey, I didn't say that." He moved his arm so it was resting across her shoulders.

"It is true, though, isn't it?"

"Well, Jelaine and James are adults. It's not as though they need me there all the time."

"I guess I've been selfish, wanting to find you. I should have realized." Her voice dissolved into tears.

His arm pulled her closer, but he didn't speak.

"I'm so sorry, Garek."

"Please don't be. I feel like I've received something good in return, meeting you."

"Honestly?"

"Yes."

They sat in silence again for what seemed a long time. At last, she felt she had to say something. "Did you say your son is named James?"

He nodded.

"You know, I had a friend—actually a lover—in my own time named James. And, come to think of it, you remind me of him."

"Really!" There was a note of bright surprise in his voice. "James was an old family name."

"Perhaps my James in the Twenty-first Century is your however many great-great-grandfather."

"Wouldn't that be something?"

"Yeah, and it means perhaps I've slept with my own great-great-great-whatever-grandfather."

"I don't think that's a close enough relationship to worry about."

"Still, it seems sort of creepy."

"Well, you had no way of knowing." He was chuckling now.

"Guess so."

"I think I should tell you I do have some feelings for your mother. Perhaps the story is true—that she was somehow in Martina's body, and I sensed her—because I do feel there's something between us now, too."

"Yeah, I couldn't believe their whole crazy story, at first." She felt her throat closing again, and had to stop talking.

After a few moments, he asked, "Are you okay?"

She shook her head. "I'm thinking of all the mistakes I've made in relationships."

"I've had my share of heart-aches, too."

"Mine are all my own fault, though. I turned my back on the one who really loved me, my boyfriend David—and went instead to other men's arms and beds. I thought I was being so independent—a strong woman. But one-by-one, they betrayed me. I guess it was God's way of punishing me for trying to run away from him, and for betraying David."

"Do you think this Lord your mother talks about is like that? If so, then I'm in trouble, too."

"Actually, I don't really know what God is like anymore. I was taught that he loves us unconditionally, and his Son died to win us forgiveness. But I'm finding it hard to forgive myself for all the wrong things I've done."

"Me, too, actually. Perhaps that's the reason I want to be with your mother, so I can try to make up for some of my past."

"I don't think Mom would want you to feel that way. She's the one person I know who seems to be able to forgive and forget. She has a good heart, and I really love her for it."

"Ginna *is* a really good person, I can tell. She's like a breath of fresh air."

"Yes, Mom's like no one else I've ever met. She put up with a lot of rebellion from me, and yet she still loves me."

"That sounds like what Martina says about your God."

"But Mom really deserves someone who loves her, just for her. Not for something that happened twenty-five or more years ago."

"Then, I'm not sure I can be that person."

"You know, what I think I need is to go to the Fountain in the Desert, the one Martina, Jael, and Jon talk about."

"What's that?" He was looking at her with a very puzzled gaze.

"Well, supposedly—while Mom and my Uncle Danny were 'within' them—they found this fountain which washes away all your past mistakes. And an old man, Eli, took them to see what Heaven is like."

"Wow, that sounds pretty far-fetched."

"Yeah, it reminds me of an old hymn that had a musical revival in my time. It says, 'There is a fountain filled with blood, drawn from the Savior's veins. And sinners plunged beneath that flood lose all their guilty stains'."

"Hmm. It almost sounds disgusting—a fountain

filled with blood. But the idea of real forgiveness—that sounds like something I need."

"Well, Mom told me it was the most wonderful water she'd ever drunk. It didn't taste like blood at all—even though it looked like it. And it made her feel like she was going to be happy forever."

"This whole thing is sounding more exotic by the minute," he laughed. "But I'd be curious to see it, if I had the chance."

"I know you weren't brought up like I was, believing in Kristos, as they call him here. Since I've been with these Believers, I feel so unworthy. Here they are giving up everything in order to stand up for their faith—a faith I used to have and then turned my back on."

"Yeah well, speaking of giving up things, I think I miss central heat the most right now," he chuckled.

"Me too! And real mattresses to sleep on, and fast food."

"What's that?"

"Oh, you know, pizza, hamburgers, French fries."

"Well, I'm not sure that stuff is still around in my world."

"You probably have other kinds of fast food now. But being here makes me feel other things are more important than the everyday stuff I miss. I think we need to experience this Fountain for ourselves, Garek—uh, Dad—is it okay if I call you that?"

"It's fine," he nodded. "So, do you know how to find this place?"

"No, but maybe Celestia can help us."

"You and Celestia seem to always find ways to get into mischief," he laughed.

"I could say it runs in the family, but she and I aren't actually related."

"Assuming I'm your father, and not Jon."

"I know, Mom has wondered, since Martina slept with you only once, but several times with Jon, when Mom was—"

"Hey, you don't need to go into all the details. Still, there are those blue eyes of yours."

"If Jon's real father—who he never met—had blue eyes, then he could have a recessive gene, and that could show up in me."

Just then he stood and reached down his hand to help her up. "I've made my choice already, Annemarie. You are *my* daughter, whether you want me or not."

"I never meant I didn't want you." She found herself hugging him tightly. "You're just what I always imagined a father would be."

"Wow, what a compliment! You're overestimating me, though."

They stood there, hugging tightly for a few more seconds. Then he released her, but took her by the hand, and began leading her back toward the stockade.

"I think we should go talk to Celestia about this Fountain," he said.

***

Celestia was watching her father's eyes, as he worked at hoeing some weeds in the small garden near the back of the stockade. It was too small for vegetables, but several herb beds were there. These helped to make the food taste better, and some also had healing properties. Right now, they were just clearing out the growth from last summer, so the herbs would have more space when they came up with the spring.

When Jon looked up at her, she quickly resumed chopping at the weeds, not wanting him to think she was slacking. After several more minutes of hoeing, Jon stopped and mopped his brow with a handkerchief. Setting down his hoe, he picked up the water bottle, and offered it to his daughter first. "Here, take a break. For so early in the spring, this sun is very warm."

"I don't mind, Dad," she laughed. "It feels good to be hot—after all the snow we had this winter."

Jon seated himself on a log set alongside the garden patch. She joined him there. "Are you still angry with me, Dad?"

He looked at her sidelong. "Well, I can't say I'm totally happy with you. After all, this is twice you've taken off without telling anyone. I know you meant well, but—"

"Dad, you know how Annemarie felt—not knowing who her father might be."

Jon shrugged. He didn't want to open that old wound again so soon.

"Well, so far you've disrupted three lives—Ginna's, Annemarie's, and Garek's. Do you feel it was justified?"

"I think you'll have to ask them that question, Dad." She nodded with her head in the direction of Garek and Annemarie, who were walking toward them, hand in hand.

"Well, they do seem happy," he admitted. "But what about Ginna?"

In recent days, Celestia reflected, Ginna was withdrawn into herself more and more. She joined them at the Gatherings, but otherwise seemed to find ways to hide herself behind a book she was reading. Other times, they'd see her gazing off into the distance with a blank look on her face. Martina tried to engage her in conversation a few times, but with very little luck.

By this time, the other two were within earshot of them.

"Hi, Celestia!" Annemarie called. "Hi, Jon!" They soon joined them on another log beside the garden. "Are you two busy?"

"Just taking a break," she replied.

Jon nodded. He still found it slightly uncomfortable

being in Garek's presence, knowing what had happened between this man and his wife. Garek was glancing down at the ground often, as though he also felt this tension.

"We really want to know more about the Fountain in the Desert," said Annemarie, deciding to get right to the point. "Both of us feel we need its cleansing—based on what we've heard from Mom and Martina about it."

"Well, it *is* a very special place," Jon said. "But also a long way from here—in a very hazardous area. I'm not sure it would be worth the risks."

"It's worth anything to me to find forgiveness," Garek said suddenly. "I need to forgive myself for taking something that wasn't mine—and I need you to forgive me, too, Jon."

Jon was taken aback at this. 'So Garek is seeing things in a new light. Perhaps being here in the camp is a good thing for him, after all.' He glanced sidelong at his daughter, and saw her smiling at him, as if to say, 'See, Dad, it *was* a good thing I did.'

"I know I need it," Annemarie was saying. "I've let my life slide down a long, slippery slope. I know I need to get right with my mother, and with the Lord—maybe even see if there's a way to find David—though I know that will probably be impossible."

"The Book says nothing is impossible for the Lord," said Celestia.

Jon nodded. He'd said this many times before. Once

it had been to Danny and Ginna—right before he'd started this grand 'experiment'—which led to all the mess they
faced now. This realization hit him like a large log across
the face. In fact, he stood and began to pace back and
forth.

Celestia could tell her father was upset, but didn't
know what to say.

Then he stopped and looked her directly in the eye. "I
owe you an apology, daughter. I've been putting the blame
on you for this situation, but I was actually the one who
caused it, when I decided to bring Ginna into Martina's
mind. I shouldn't have played with people's lives like that."

She stood and gave him a hug. "Dad, don't beat
yourself up. You had no way of knowing all this would
happen."

"Yes, please," added Annemarie. "There's no point
in looking back. We need to find ways to move on from
here."

"That's why we want to know about the Fountain,"
said Garek.

Jon sat back down, and his daughter joined him. He
shook his head, and scratched his hands together, hearing
the scrape of the rough calluses on them, before he began
to speak.

"When I was young," he sighed, "I thought I knew
what my destiny was: to pilot ships all over the Galaxy, a
life among the stars. But when I fell in love with Martina,

I knew I needed to try to understand this God her family thought was so important. Part of the motivation was so I could be worthy of her."

"She felt unworthy of you, too, Dad."

"I know. Ironic, isn't it? Still, between the two of us, we tried to work it out—and knew we had to find this Fountain. It seemed to be the only way we were going to be okay in each other's eyes—and in the Lord's eyes, too."

"I'm afraid I helped complicate some of that," Garek said softly. "That's one of my regrets. And after Martina, there were other women in my life."

"I have the same problem," Annemarie sighed. "I made a mess of my love life, too. I don't know if either of you have ever felt this desperate need to be cleansed."

Celestia was looking at her friend intently, but made no move.

"Actually, I did—many times," Jon said. "I was deep into the Terres Underground before I met Martina. I realized one day I was as corrupt and filthy as my unknown father, and unworthy of the parents who tried to love me."

His voice broke. No one spoke, and all four tried to breathe softly—somehow hoping they wouldn't be the one to interrupt this precarious moment.

At last, Celestia sighed, "I guess I'm the only one here who's still a virgin, but I have mistakes I regret, too."

Then Garek spoke up, "So, Jon, what can you tell us about this Fountain?"

"Only that I've never been to any place like it. And once I bathed in it and drank of its waters, I knew I'd never be the same again. My life was turned around, somehow."

"My church taught 'repentance' means 'to turn around'—away from your past," said Annemarie.

"Yes, I understand that now," Jon nodded. "Somehow, once you've experienced repentance at this Fountain, you never want to go back to the life you had before. You still make mistakes, but you know you somehow belong to the Lord, and he will never let you stray too far from him."

"Sort of like sheep?" said Garek.

Jon looked at him in surprise. "Yes, that's a comparison The Book uses often. Have you read it?"

"No, but maybe something Martina once told me is still there in my head."

Jon looked even more surprised now. "Martina talked to you about The Book and the True Lord?"

"Oh, absolutely! Often, in fact. In her last letter, that's all she talked about—how she felt God wanted her to stay with you."

Jon was silent, surprised to hear this. Perhaps he'd been harder on his wife than he should have. Now his respect for her began to grow again. And he was beginning to see this man beside him as another human who was searching—just as he had been, all those years ago.

"I was one of those people who had to see for myself to believe," Jon said then.

"Like doubting Thomas?" asked Annemarie.

"Exactly. You've read his story, too?"

"It's taught in church every year, Jon—just after Easter," she laughed.

"Easter? What's that?" asked Celestia.

"It's the time of the year when we remember the Lord's death and resurrection," she said.

"We remember that at every Gathering," said Jon.

"Well, it gets a lot of telling in my time, too. But especially at Easter—it's an important holiday—or it used to be. In my time, it's getting dragged down into a lot of commercialism. And the religious aspect tends to be ignored."

"The way the whole thing is ignored in this world," Celestia nodded.

"Anyway," Jon resumed, smiling at the way the conversation kept wandering in new directions. "As I was saying, I needed to experience this forgiveness, or cleansing—or whatever you want to call it—for myself. Your Uncle Darien," he nodded to his daughter, "was blessed to be one of those who took God at his Word and believed, but not me, I'm afraid."

" 'Blessed are those who have not seen, and yet have believed.' That's what the Lord told Thomas, when he showed him his wounded hands and side," added Annemarie.

"This is getting really deep for me," Garek suddenly put in.

Jon glanced over at the man, and was surprised to see something of his old self in those blue eyes. Almost without realizing what he was doing, he reached out and patted him on the back. "I remember how that feels, Garek. Really, I do."

They all lapsed into silence again.

Finally, Celestia turned to her father and touched his arm gently. "Dad?"

"Yes, I know. We have to try. We'll find a way to take you to the Fountain."

CHAPTER 13

CALM BEFORE THE STORM

Annemarie was wandering the woods near the edge of the meadow, as she often did. Her mind was in a whirl again because she didn't seem to know what to do with herself. Now that Jon said he'd try to find the Fountain, all she wanted to do was get there.

Instead, Darien cautioned them to wait. "There's been a big increase in Patrols lately," he said. "Drones have been seen very close to here, too. It's not safe for us to head for any of the cities right now."

'But all I can think of is finding relief from my messed-up life,' she thought, almost speaking aloud. The sound of the wind in the trees was becoming louder now, like the sound of rain pounding on a metal roof—something she hadn't heard since they'd left Colorado. 'I'm not ready to face my own world yet—that's for sure,' she sighed. 'I have a lot of soul-repair to do first.'

Just then, she saw a tan-colored shape through the tree trunks, and stopped dead in her tracks. Was it a soldier? She knew she wasn't supposed to be out here alone—everyone had been warned to never travel with fewer than five people.

After standing frozen to a tree for several minutes, she began to hear a voice above the sighing of the wind. To her relief she recognized it as Celestia, who was kneeling with her hands raised up toward the sky, praying, "Oh Lord, I know you've told me to help Annemarie and Ginna, so I brought them here. But what should I do next? Ginna seems shy of Garek, and Annemarie still doesn't fully understand your forgiveness."

'What does she mean?' Annemarie thought.

Then Celestia's voice went on, "Lord, I know your grace is open to all. And I think Ginna understands this. But Garek and Annemarie think they need to do something themselves to be worthy of you—like going to the Fountain."

Annemarie began to feel angry. 'Of course, I need to do something!' she thought. 'I need to clean up my messy life, but I don't know how.'

She found herself stalking up to Celestia and pulling on one of her hands. "What are you doing?" she demanded.

Celestia's deep brown eyes looked up at her, and she was surprised to see tears in them. Slowly her friend rose to her feet.

"I was talking to the one whose orders I follow," she sighed. "Remember back in Colorado when you asked me about that?"

"Your orders are from the Lord? I thought you meant some person sent you."

"Well, he is a personal God, Annemarie. What you need to do is get to know him better."

"I used to think I knew God." Annemarie leaned against the rough bark of the nearest tree. "But now I feel like there's a huge wall between us, or a gorge too steep for anyone to cross. Mom says Martina and Jon didn't really understand the Lord until they found the Fountain. I guess I must be like them," she sighed, brushing at her eyes. "I have to go there."

Celestia nodded, but didn't speak. In her heart she thought, 'I wish there was some way to help her see that faith doesn't always need physical evidence. 'Lord, help me know what to say.'

But still they stood in silence, and the only sound was the wind.

"The wind blows where it wills, and so it is with the Spirit of God," Annemarie's voice murmured.

Celestia turned to her in surprise. "Where did you hear that? It's from The Book."

Annemarie smiled slightly. "I used to read it when I was a child. But now I'm not sure I really understood it."

"Perhaps you understand more than you realize,

Annemarie. I think you should just try praying, you know, talking to the Lord more."

"I guess you're right," she sighed deeply. "But it never seems like he's there anymore. I feel like I'm talking to emptiness."

"The Book also says he told his followers, 'I will never leave you or forsake you.' So don't give up—he's still there for you."

"I hope so."

A sudden blast of cold wind hit them just then, and both women pulled their jackets more tightly around them.

"Looks like the weather is changing," said Celestia loudly, above the wind's sound. "We'd better get back to camp."

***

As soon as they reached the compound, Jon met them, his lips drawn into a thin, angry line. "You two shouldn't be wandering like this."

"I'm sorry, Dad. I just needed some time alone with the Lord—to pray."

"I know there's no place to really be alone here in the compound," he sighed. "Did you have any new revelations?"

"Dad, don't make it sound like that. I'm getting some sort of messages or signals from the Lord—like when I knew I had to go save Annemarie from herself."

Annemarie shuffled her feet and stared at the ground, not sure what to say.

"I suppose that's why you two took off without permission—against Darien's orders, in fact—to try to find Garek." added Jon.

Celestia sighed. Dad just didn't seem to quite understand this connection she had—this mission she knew she must fulfill.

"I know you feel you have a calling, daughter," he was saying. "But as your father, my concern is your safety."

She took his hand. "I understand, Dad. And I'm always trying to be careful."

Annemarie kept looking back and forth at the two of them, not sure what all this was about. "I was the one wandering alone. I'm sorry, Jon," she said at last.

"Dad, I believe I need to get Garek and Annemarie to the Fountain as soon as possible. There's a feeling in the air something bad is about to happen that could block the whole plan."

Jon sighed deeply and shrugged. The wind was getting stronger and colder now. "Let's talk more tomorrow," he said. "I need to gather wood for our fire, before this storm really sets in."

Celestia nodded, but she was feeling a sense of urgency she couldn't seem to suppress. Events would soon prove her correct.

CHAPTER 14

SPRING BREAKUP

Ginna lay on her sleeping mat listening to the wind whipping rain against the sides and roof of Darien's hut. This storm came so suddenly that it was frightening her. But, we'll let her tell it herself:

The wind was howling around us, making the hut shudder. I burrowed into my blanket but couldn't sleep. As usual, I was feeling guilty for being a burden to people who were living on the edge in these turbulent times. But then I reflected how often it was the people with fewer material possessions who were more generous toward strangers in need.

'Perhaps when you depend on the Lord each and every day just to get by, you realize what is really important in life—your relationships,' I thought.

This was a revelation for me, because I'd lived so much of my life isolating myself. All those years when I couldn't face the people of my school, church, or town—the years when I couldn't bear their judgmental looks and snide remarks. Now I felt like weeping for all that wasted time.

'But, what could I have done differently?' I wondered. 'Maybe a stronger person than me would have done better.'

A few days before, Daiah had told me more details of her life here, as we worked together putting in a garden:

"At first, we were tolerated, Ginna," she said. "But soon the news media, and the Union government began labeling us as Rebel supporters and obstructionists, because we believe what The Book says—that Kristos is the only way to really come to faith in the True Lord."

" 'No one comes to the Father, but by me.' Kristos said that, didn't he?" I asked.

She nodded. "And he also said, 'I am the way, the truth, and the life,'."

"Many in my own time are beginning to call Christian believers narrow-minded," I added. "We're sometimes accused of racism, too. Some seem to think our God is only a 'white man's god'."

"If we're really doing what The Book teaches, though, we should be accepting of all people, because the Lord created all and came to Earth to save everyone."

"What happened to you Believers next?" I asked, stopping to rest my back for a few moments.

"Well, it was gradual. First people began to burn our books, but we managed to keep some hidden."

"Martina told me about things like that happening on Terres."

"I saw the same. I lived on Terres for much of my early life, you know."

"That's right. I'd forgotten."

"Anyway, after this, they began denying us access to credit so we couldn't buy anything in the stores anymore. People were required to have a credit chip embedded in their wrist, but Believers weren't permitted to get one, even if we'd been willing to."

I tried to imagine what this must have been like. In my own life, I would have felt totally lost if I couldn't get my groceries—or any other items—at the local store. "What did you do?"

"Well, we Believers began trading and bartering with each other, since we were all in the same boat, so to speak. Then they exiled us from the cities altogether."

"Martina and I met Kai and Elias, who were still try-ing to exist in Tornatoh."

"Yes, a few have held on for awhile. But their days are numbered, I think. So here we are, trying to live off the land."

"It seems like a lot of hard work," I said, trying to stretch an ache out of my back. My knees were also protesting.

Daiah smiled. "It *is* work, but at least we're staying strong and getting lots of fresh air."

"Yeah, you're probably healthier than a lot of people in my time."

"We have to be careful of dietary deficiencies, though. It isn't always possible to get the right nutrients, especially in winter."

"So you're glad to see the spring, I bet."

"For sure! It helps me feel more hopeful as I see the forests and the fields coming back to life."

"I remember feeling that way, too. The sun climbs higher in the sky, the days get longer, the plants begin to green-up. It just lifts my spirits."

"Back when we still had groundcars, though, we had to be careful of places where the roads began to fall apart."

"I remember that from my own time in Colorado," I laughed. "The farm trucks and log trucks would hit places where the pavement was beginning to crack, and their weight would cause the cracks and holes to get bigger and bigger each day. Soon parts of the road would be nothing but mud holes, with pulverized pieces of asphalt in them. We called it 'Spring Breakup'."

"Springs can be like that here in our time, too."

"Are you glad you left Terres?"

"Oh, yes! Life may be hard here, but I can't imagine living as I did before with the Redlarks."

"I never experienced that life firsthand—only what Martina remembered, which is sort of patchy."

"I'm not surprised," she nodded. "Martina had a

rough time there, and it's a blessing she doesn't remember all of it. Say, Ginna, what are you and Annemarie going to do now?"

I turned and looked at her. The wind was blowing the short, curly ends of my hair into my eyes. I brushed them back, but it was a futile gesture. "Daiah, I really don't know yet," I sighed.

We went back to hoeing and breaking up the soil so it would be more pliable for planting. "With more Patrols and Drones reported in the vicinity, the garden plots have to be smaller than before," she said. "And we also need to shelter them from view, by putting them under the eaves of the forest."

"Will things grow in this shade?" I asked.

"Probably not as well," she sighed. "But whatever produce we get is better than nothing."

"Don't you ever get discouraged or frightened by all this?"

"Sure. We all get down at times. But it seems to me that as the world grows cold toward us, we draw together, finding warmth in our care for each other, and in the light of the Lord and his love."

***

Now, as I lay listening to the storm outside, I knew what she meant. We were here in a dry, warm place—together—while the forces of the world raged around us.

The wind was getting stronger now. I could hear it racing through the pines and other evergreens just beyond the stockade fence. It seemed as though heavy sheets of water were lashing against the walls, and I felt thankful I was inside, only listening and not feeling the full force of the storm.

Garek had moved to another hut when I was released from the Infirmary. With Alexia and Andre, there wasn't enough room for two extra people in Darien's hut. Part of me felt a sense of relief to not be sleeping so close to Garek. I could sense his attraction to me, but I just wasn't sure how I felt about him yet.

Annemarie and Celestia actually were at the Torova's now, as they were supposed to have been all along, and Jon and Martina were still at Jael's. I sensed restlessness in Jon, though. He was probably feeling we needed to get back to their cave and the cache of meat before it went bad. It went without saying no food should be wasted if it could be helped. And with spring coming, their cool room would be too warm soon.

Again, I realized my daughter and I were part of the problem. She and Garek had asked to be taken to the Fountain in the Desert—and Jon had agreed. And this meant he was tied down here until this trip was figured out.

Restlessly, I rolled onto my side, trying to think of something to do about it. Perhaps I could help them cross the GAP—and so could Celestia. Even Annemarie and Garek had this power, but none of us had Jon's training and experience, so I understood his hesitation to let us go alone. And I knew he didn't like the idea of his daughter taking us by herself. There seemed to be no answer, so I tried again to sleep.

When dawn came at last, the rain had stopped. The only sounds now were the *plop-plops* of drips from the trees, hitting the hut's roof. I rose as soon as I saw the first light coming in around the door, but Daiah was already up, building a small cooking fire. I moved to help her, wanting to be of any use that I could.

We'd barely started sipping our herb tea when the ground seemed to rumble. Our eyes grew wide in surprise.

"Is that thunder?" I asked. "I thought the storm was over."

"More likely an earthquake, by the feel of it," said Darien, leaping from his bed.

Just then, a loud explosion overpowered the rumbling sound. "That's no earthquake!" Daiah shouted.

Jon's head appeared at the hut's door. "It's heavy armor—tanks and walking-howitzers!" he shouted. "A Drone just hit north of the stockade. We're being attacked!"

"Sound the alarm bell!" Darien cried. "Everyone knows what they're supposed to do. The soldiers will assemble to hold them off, if we can. The rest of the women will take charge of evacuating the camp."

"How did they find us?" asked Daiah. "We've done our best to keep hidden."

Jon just shrugged, and he and Darien ran out the door.

I was wondering about her question myself. Had our presence tipped someone off? More likely—now that I thought of it—the disappearance of Garek, Celestia, and Annemarie from their prison cell in Tornatoh must have triggered increased System awareness of our presence, so-called Safe-Zone or not.

By this time, Daiah had smothered the fire, and was stuffing what food would travel into a pack-sack. I tried to do the same. Outside the hut, we could hear shouts of men and women giving orders. There was no panic, though. It seemed this evacuation had been rehearsed well.

Across the compound, I saw Splash rearing and heard him whinny in fear. I wished I could go to him, but Daiah was pulling me in the opposite direction. All I could do was hope Jael would reach his horse in time to help.

Then another explosion kicked up clouds of dust and smoke, and Splash faded from my sight. To myself, I thought a silent prayer for his safety, though at the back of my mind, I wondered if it was all right to pray for a horse.

Soon I had no more time for prayers or thoughts, as Daiah guided me down a narrow path that ran along the stockade wall. She didn't stop until she reached a small door partly hidden by the low-hanging branches of a spruce tree growing just outside the log wall.

She paused a moment to catch her breath, which I sorely needed, too. In another minute, we were joined by Celestia and Annemarie.

"Everyone is divided into their assigned Scatter Groups," said Celestia, between gasps for breath. "We're glad we found you."

"Alexia and Andre?" Daiah barely breathed her children's names. I felt a desperate knot lodge in my throat, knowing how I'd feel if I didn't know where my child was.

"They're with Jael and Raina, who are in charge of all the children," nodded Celestia. "The plan is working well, so far."

"Okay, we have to get moving—right now."

Without another word, Daiah pushed the small door open, and the four of us crawled through. We moved as quickly and quietly as possible into the silent early morning forest. I had no idea which direction we were going, but just kept following Daiah. Celestia was at her side by now. I reached over and grabbed my daughter's hand.

"What are we doing here, Mom?"

"Seeing what the future holds for Believers, I guess."

"I wish we could just go back."

"Let's talk later," I gasped, too short of breath to talk and run at the same time. Just then we heard a buzzing sound above our heads. Something looking like a metal dragonfly dipped and dodged in front of us. We managed to get a bit farther before a large explosion behind us split the air. I found myself flat on the ground before I even knew what happened.

"Mom! Are you all right?"

I nodded shakily and managed to get to my feet.

"This way—quickly!" called Celestia. "Before any more Drones spot us."

I couldn't see anything through the smoke and haze, so I just stumbled along toward the sound of her voice.

Soon, we saw a large, ancient-looking oak looming before us. Near the base, back in a tangle of roots, was a small opening. As we crawled inside, I could feel hanging bits of moss and spiders' webs clinging to my face and hair. Halfway shuddering, I kept reminding myself this place was safer than out there in the battle.

"Where are we?" I heard Annemarie whisper.

"Sh!" Daiah tapped her sharply on the shoulder. "Not far enough away to be safe—that's where we are."

In stunned silence, we huddled in the damp darkness of the tree's roots. Closing my eyes, I tried to think of visualizations to keep my mind off the danger. 'When we were kids, Danny would have loved finding a place like this,' I thought. It seemed to help me calm a bit to think of my younger brother. 'He would've wanted to build a fort or hideout here.' I smiled to myself, imagining Danny nestled next to me, perhaps telling one of his made-up adventure stories. 'So here we are, and it *is* a good hideout, I hope,' I sighed to myself.

Things seemed to have gone quiet above us. I wasn't sure if this was good or bad, so I tapped Celestia on the arm and motioned upward with my head, as though to ask the question in my mind.

She shook her head back at me, so I gathered silence above us could be just as dangerous as the sounds of battle.

After a few more minutes, she crept slowly back the way we'd come, poking her head out just enough to peek around. Then she quickly scooted back. "Scouts!" She merely mouthed the word.

Again, we sat in breathless silence for what seemed like eternity. Then we heard the sound of boots crunching in the dry leaves and forest litter right at the entrance of our hideout.

Celestia grabbed my hand, and pulled it toward Daiah's. I saw she was grouping us into a circle. "GAP!" she mouthed. "Only way…"

I wondered if anyone outside would sense our presence as we crossed the GAP, but there was no way to know for sure. Evidently Celestia had assessed the dangers and made the best choice she could.

The next moment, the ground was falling away beneath me. After an instant of seeming nothingness around us, I began to feel cool rock under my thighs. Now we were in a dark place with rock walls. After glancing around a little more, I began to recognize the cave we'd stayed in with Jon and Martina, when we'd first come to this world.

"I hope your parents will find their way here, too, Celestia."

She nodded, but seemed too out of breath to speak.

All of sudden, I felt an overwhelming fatigue washing over me. I sank lower, leaning my head against the stone wall behind me, trying to keep the world from spinning around.

"Are you okay, Ginna?" I barely heard Daiah's words and tried to nod. Looking up, I saw her face begin to come back into focus.

"I'll be all right—just got dizzy there all of a sudden." Why was I always the one getting faint or passing out?

Celestia handed me a cup of some cool liquid, which I sipped gratefully.

Just then, there came a crackly sound on our left, and figures began to emerge from a haze. I fervently hoped they weren't enemy soldiers who followed us. Fortunately, I soon made out the forms of Jon and Martina, who were supporting a third person between them.

"Mom! Dad!" Celestia sounded very relieved.

"I hope we haven't brought trouble along with us," sighed Jon, as they laid the third person gently on the cave floor.

Now I saw that it was Garek, and he appeared to be unconscious. Slowly I moved toward him, taking his hand.

"Did Darien get away?" I could hear the fear in Daiah's voice.

"Yes, he took his established safety route," said Jon.

"Did you see Andre and Alexia?"

"Everyone made it to their assigned group, and as far as I know, all were safely evacuated. The soldiers running the diversion left just after the women and children. The only great loss is our food."

"Somehow, the Lord will provide for us," whispered Martina.

A moaning sound began beside me, and Garek's hand clutched at mine. Then he sat up abruptly, throwing his arms in front of his face in a protective gesture.

"Hey, you're safe here," I said, pulling his arms gently down.

"Where am I?"

"In a cave," I said, not sure if I was permitted to tell him anything else. "Here, drink some of this." I handed him my half-empty cup. Whatever was in it had revived me, so I hoped it would do the same for him.

"What happened?" he asked, after he drained the cup.

"We were surprise attacked," said Martina. "Jon and I were running a diversion, while our camp evacuated. Just before we crossed the GAP, you stumbled into us. There must have been a Drone explosion nearby, because all three of us were thrown into the air. When we landed, I grabbed both you and Jon, and told him to cross immediately."

"Which I did."

"So, it appears I've joined you—for better or worse," sighed Garek.

"You'd surely be branded a Rebel if you tried to go back now," said Jon.

I looked from Jon to Garek and saw some of the animosity between them fading. As I did this, I noticed the deep gash on Garek's left arm. "Does anyone have a bandage or something?" I asked. "Look, he's hurt."

Martina pulled something from her pocket looking like an oversized handkerchief. I took it without a word, and bound it around the wound.

"Probably took some shrapnel," said Jon.

When I'd finished, I saw Garek looking into my eyes. I looked down, though, not ready for *any* more emotions right now.

Jon turned to Daiah. "Thanks for gathering my family, Daiah. I couldn't do the same for you, I'm afraid, but I'll pray they're all safe."

"Actually, Celestia and Annemarie found *us*," I said, seeing Daiah was too overcome to speak just then. "It was Celestia who found the hiding place for us in the old oak."

"I remembered playing in it when I was younger," she smiled.

I nodded, realizing this was just what I'd been thinking

when we were there, deep in the tree's roots. "She's also the one who crossed the GAP with us when the Scouts got too close," I added.

Jon turned and smiled proudly at his daughter. "Well done! You're more of a soldier than I realized."

Celestia merely shrugged and said, "Thanks, Dad. I guess I take after you."

***

Toward evening, or so it seemed from inside the cave, we all managed to eat some of the stew Martina and Daiah made from Jon's beaver. It definitely had a strong, gamey taste, but we were so famished from all the anxiety and activity that I think anything would have tasted good right then.

As we were settling down to sleep, each in the most level spot we could find, and rolled in whatever blanket or clothing was available for warmth, I turned to Martina:

"I understand how you felt in the Valley now."

"What?" I could tell her mind was totally confused.

"You know, when you were trying to decide between Jon and Garek."

"Oh?" Her eyes showed this was the last thing she'd expected me to talk about. "What do you mean?"

I could feel my face beginning to burn. Perhaps I shouldn't be telling her any of my thoughts on this subject, but I'd bottled it up inside for much too long, all my adult life, in fact.

"Well, you knew you loved Jon, and yet you also had feelings for Garek, so you were trying to decide what to do with them—right?"

"Yeah, I guess so. It's been a long time since I thought much about it—well up until Celestia brought you two here."

"I'm not sure how to explain, but I think I had the same feelings. I mean, I care about both of them, too. But for me it's very different than for you. You made your choice and stayed with Jon. That's what I wanted, too…"

My voice caught in my throat, and tears were beginning to sting my eyes. "But I can't have Jon," I managed to add. "He's yours. Now, I think Garek has feelings for me, but I'm not sure I feel the same. If I was to be with him—the way you're with Jon—I think it might be like living a lie. I don't really know what to do."

Silence overwhelmed me then. I regretted exposing my feelings to her, but there was relief, too. Now I didn't have to keep them bottled up inside me anymore. She reached over and squeezed my hand. "I'm glad you feel you can be so honest with me, Ginna. I don't know what to tell you to do, though."

"I guess we'll just have to wait and see," I sighed.

***

As the next few days went by, we kept close to the cave and stayed out of sight as much as we could. It wasn't long before we were feeling very cooped up. The spring weather continued, and this made it twice as hard to stay in the cave, missing out on hours of warm sunshine outdoors.

Daiah kept wishing she could go back to planting her garden, but we hadn't found a safe place for a plot here. I wondered how she could function at all, not knowing for sure where the rest of her family was. I didn't want to ask her, though, and risk upsetting her more.

Garek seemed to be recovering from his wound for the first couple of days. But on the morning of the third day, he was feverish and listless.

"It looks like he's gotten an infection," Martina sighed.

"What can we do?" I asked, knowing that the antiseptics and antibiotics of my world, and this one, were no longer available to the outcast Believers.

"It's too early for the witch hazel to be in leaf," she said. "I might have some dried in our storage, though. It's only an astringent, but perhaps it will help."

Soon she found some dried leaves which she boiled in water. Then she soaked a cloth in the liquid, and we bound it to the wound. "Tomorrow, we can sponge his arm with it again," she added.

By this time, he seemed to have slipped into semi-consciousness. "Isn't there anything else I can do?" I asked.

"Just put this cool compress on his forehead, and pray."

And I did, for hours on end, sitting there beside him and wiping his feverish brow, praying somehow he would be spared. I wasn't sure what I felt for him anymore. There really was no room left in my mind for more emotions or decisions.

Early the next morning, Martina came over to my side. "Ginna, please go get some sleep. I'll come get you if anything changes."

I looked up at her blankly and slowly got up. Soon I was crawling into my blanket, and fell asleep almost instantly.

When I woke, the light was fading into evening again. To my surprise, Jon was the one keeping vigil beside Garek. "Where's Martina?"

"She went out to help Daiah find some more herbs. They think they know something else that will help."

"Won't it be dark soon?"

"This was a safer time for them to go. They'll be harder for any possible Scouts or Drones to spot."

"Jon, I feel terrible about all this."

"Please don't, Ginna."

I knew I shouldn't sit close to him, but found myself doing it anyway. "This is all my fault, you know. If I hadn't come back, you'd all still be together in your Safe-Zone, Garek would be in his own world, and I'd be in mine. Instead I let myself hope something good would happen to me for a change, and now all these bad things have happened to everyone—because of me."

"Sh, now." He reached his arm around my shoulders.

I found myself leaning into his embrace, weeping onto his shirt. It was the first time I'd felt cared for, in a very long time. But then I pulled back, knowing I was taking advantage of him. I had no right to rest in this man's arms, I told myself. He wasn't mine.

"What's wrong? Ginna, what did I do?" He could tell I'd pulled away on purpose.

"I shouldn't take advantage of you like this, Jon. I need you so much, but it would be wrong for me to take from you what's rightfully Martina's."

"I'm just trying to let you know we care about you, Ginna. And any of these things might still have happened, even if you hadn't come. You need to stop blaming yourself."

Tears were streaming down my cheeks again. I wished my tear ducts would just dry up. I was tired of being the one who often burst into tears.

"I'm sorry, Jon. You're a kind and good man, and I know you all care about me. I just don't want you to keep trying to make up for what happened twenty-five years ago. What's done is done. No one can go back and change it. You and Martina got married, and I went back to my world—and had a daughter. There's nothing we can do about it now."

"Yes, you *are* right, Ginna. And you need to do the same. You need to quit trying to make things up to Garek. Like you say, what's done is done."

I stared at him in silence for a few minutes. Then I let him take my hands in his, as he slowly drew me into a hug.

"You know the Lord loves you more than any human being could, don't you?"

I nodded mutely.

"Let's just trust he will give his children—us—the best things he can."

"The way we try to give the best to our own children," I whispered.

"Even if we don't have all the good things in this world that we'd like, we still have Heaven to look forward to. Remember?"

"Yes, Jon, I do remember what Heaven was like when Eli took us there. It was like nothing I'd ever experienced before, or since. I was so filled with the most unspeakable joy."

"How can I not want that for everyone I know? Even for Garek," he whispered.

"All the more reason to pray for him to recover, so we can help him see," I sighed.

"And you know, if you and Annemarie hadn't come here, Garek would never have been here with us Believers."

"I never thought of it that way."

"See, the Lord's ways are not like ours. 'As far as the

heavens are above the earth, so are my thoughts higher than your thoughts,' he said."

"No wonder he seems so mysterious and inscrutable sometimes."

I was still leaning on him, his arm around my shoulders beside Garek's still form when the others came back.

Martina smiled when she saw us and didn't seem at all disturbed. I realized she knew her husband well enough to tell when he was just trying to help a friend. This took a great load off me, and I found myself smiling back at her.

Soon she and Daiah were brewing a new tea with a very strong medicinal smell. "Well, this sure smells like a hospital," I said.

Daiah smiled up at me. "We found all the herbs we were looking for. Hopefully this will help." She handed me a damp cloth she'd poured some of the liquid onto. "Put this on his forehead until we can get him to drink something."

For the rest of that night, we took turns sitting vigil, putting the freshly-dipped compresses on his head.

My second watch was near morning. Just as I put a newly dipped cloth on his head, I noticed his blue eyes were open and looking up at me. "Are you an angel?" his shaky voice rasped.

CHAPTER 15

COMING TO TERMS

Garek was by no means out of danger, but each day he seemed a bit better than the last. Each of us women took a turn helping him sip the medicinal brew Daiah and Martina made. After a few more days, he grew strong enough to sit up and swallow a little soup I spooned into his mouth.

He had little strength for talking, and I felt a strange sense of relief at this, for I was at a loss as to what to say to him. Part of me wanted to get to know him better, but another part of my mind kept telling me to hold back. I had very few experiences with men in my life and kept hearing myself say, 'I've made it all these years on my own. Why should I need a man now?'

And yet, I'd known some very lonely times, especially after my mother died. Why should I run from someone who wanted to get to know me—the real me? Was it because I was just stubborn? Or because I was afraid of commitment? And the biggest question, 'If Garek had known about Annemarie years ago, would he have cared enough to find her—and me—if it had been possible?'

One day, after he finished the bowl of soup I was feeding him, he grabbed my hand as I set the bowl down on the floor beside the sleeping mat. "Ginna, do you hate me for what happened?"

"What? Hate you? Of course not! How could you think such a thing?"

His eyes blinked closed for a few seconds. "Well, if I were in your place, I might hate someone who caused *me* so much pain."

"But you didn't even know. It's not as though you intended to hurt me."

"Now that I do know, though, there must be something I can do to make it up to you."

"I'm not expecting anything from you, Garek." Yet, as soon as I said this, I knew it wasn't entirely true. Otherwise, why had I come to this time?

"Can you just let me get to know you? I don't want you to feel like I'm forcing myself on you," he added.

"Well, I don't want you to feel that way, either," I sighed.

We just sat there for a long time, and neither of us moved to break the grip our hands had on each other.

"You're in a fragile place right now," he said at last.

"Here in this place—out of your own time—with none of the support system you probably have in your world."

"Well, the same can be said for you, Garek. We've taken you from your own world, too."

"So, both of us are sort of cast adrift in a strange sea, aren't we?"

I nodded, trying to keep any tears from rising in my eyes. "It seems like every time I tell myself to draw back and give you more space, something happens to throw us back together—like this."

"You know, Martina would probably say it's her Lord who keeps bringing us back together."

There was actually a slight chuckle in his voice, and when I looked at him, I could see some of the old sparkle returning to his eyes. In spite of myself, I felt a warmth when I saw this. But then I looked down, to keep from betraying too many of my own feelings.

"You need to get stronger first," I said at last. "Right now, my job is to help you get well."

"I wonder how many wounded soldiers have fallen in love with their nurses," he whispered.

"Please, Garek. Don't go there right now."

"Okay," he smiled, closing his eyes. "But I still think you're an angel."

***

Once he was strong enough to get out of bed, Annemarie and I took turns walking with him. Since no Drones or Patrols were seen recently in our vicinity, Jon and Martina were spending their time breaking ground for a garden. Celestia and Daiah helped most days, too, either with the digging or with the search for seeds to plant.

The world outside the cave had burst into spring while Garek lay inside. The warm air was heavenly, and I'd never enjoyed the sounds of birdsong more. It was surprising how many I recognized from my world, here in the future. There were blue jays, cardinals, sparrows, and goldfinches.

"Where did you learn all these bird names?" Garek asked me one day, as I helped support his weight while he walked slowly.

"Well, none of these—except the sparrows—were common in Colorado, so perhaps I'm remembering them from my childhood in Texas."

"You grew up in Texas?"

"My family lived there until I was about twelve years old."

"I spent about five years there working with the Forestry Commission."

"What part of the state?"

"Over in the pine woods in the southeast."

"We used to go camping over there—my dad and I."

"Of course, we were a few centuries apart," he chuckled.

"At least it's good to know some of what I remember still exists."

"Well, it did twenty or thirty years ago, anyway."

"And then you came to Salien, where you met Martina."

He nodded. "Working on the Resource Allocation Project. Come to think of it, that's how I 'met' you, too."

"Well, sort of," I tried to smile, and we settled into an awkward silence. "There's really no easy way to deal with this, is there, Garek?"

"Maybe you're just trying too hard, Ginna."

"But what should I do?"

"How about we pretend we've only just met?"

"That could be a little hard. After all there's Annemarie."

"Well, try not to think of her as mine. Actually, she's yours, you know—you've known her all her life, and that's something which will never be true for me."

"What do you think of her?"

He stopped walking just then. "Let's find a place to sit down."

"Are you all right?"

"Yeah, I just need to catch my breath."

We seated ourselves on a fallen log nearby in a sheltered spot.

"That's much better," he breathed.

"Should we get you back to the cave?" I was concerned with the sounds of his heavy breathing.

"No, I'll be fine. Just need to rest a bit. What were we saying?"

"I think I'd asked what you thought of your daughter." I wasn't sure how he'd react to my calling her this and was relieved when he chuckled.

"Well, I find her to be a wonderful young woman. Any man would be glad to claim her as his daughter. She and I have managed to come to a sort of agreement, that we're willing to accept each other at face value."

"So you're 'just friends,' as the saying goes?"

"No, I'd say we're a bit more than that. But I can't find the right words. For one thing, I don't mind if she wants to call me 'Dad'."

Silence settled over us for a few minutes then, like the sun slipping behind a cloud.

"Are we just friends, too?" I found myself asking.

"If that's what you want, Ginna."

As he said this, though, he'd taken my hand in his, squeezed it gently, and then rubbed his thumb across the knuckles. It was a sensation my body remembered from somewhere.

"What do you want, Garek?"

"I want you to be happy. You haven't been very happy so far in your life, have you?"

"It's been bitter along with the sweet. But I don't think I have the right to ask for more."

"Why not?"

I had no immediate answer for him but finally I sighed, "I guess I don't feel I deserve it."

"You shouldn't feel that way, Ginna." His arm was around my waist now. "You have as much right as anyone to happiness. You're a very special woman."

My insides were beginning to tremble. Part of me was aching to be closer to him, and part of me wanted to jump up and run away. Then he took my chin in his free hand, and drew my face toward his. I could feel the warmth of his breath on my cheek, and then the touch of his lips on mine. This was when I began to let go of anything inside I'd been holding back.

I'd never felt these sensations in my own skin. There had been feelings similar to this long ago, when I was part of Martina. But this was so different. The strength of his embrace and the tenderness of his touch made me feel giddy, but also calm. I found there really were no words to explain it.

He pulled back slowly, looking into my eyes. All I found I could do was reach up a trembling finger and touch his lips.

"Ginna, do you think you could learn to love me?"

I found myself nodding slowly. "I've never really been in love before," I whispered. "But I think I'm beginning to know what it feels like."

At this, he smiled and kissed me again.

CHAPTER 16

DRONE ATTACK

Just a week or two later, Daiah and I were weeding the tiny garden patch she and Martina had managed to plant. The sun was getting warmer as the morning wore on, and so I decided to ask a question to get my mind on something else:

"Say, I heard Celestia and Martina arguing the other day. They really sounded angry, but I couldn't make out their words. Do you know anything about it, Daiah?"

She looked at the ground for a moment and then took a deep breath before she spoke. "I've heard them discussing Celestia's 'callings' recently—if that's what you mean."

"What 'callings'?"

"Well, Ginna, I don't know a lot about it, but Celestia says the Lord speaks to her."

"Really? Does he ever speak to you, Daiah?"

"Not me. It seems Celestia is the only one I know

who receives these messages. One of the first was to go find Annemarie."

"And then they found me, and we came here. So Celestia said the Lord told her to do that?"

"Yes, and that's why she and Annemarie took off on their own to find Garek, too."

A cold chill ran through me suddenly, just remembering the dark damp jail cell where Martina and I found them. "At least we got them back," I sighed. "What's the problem now?"

"Celestia says she's being called to take you, Garek, and Annemarie to the Fountain."

"The True Fountain—the one I went to when I was 'within' Martina?"

"That's what I've heard them talking about."

"More like arguing, if you ask me, Daiah."

"Yeah, those two can get pretty heated, can't they? Anyway, Celestia insists she must obey her 'calling.' But Martina doesn't want her to go without Jon along. She's afraid Celestia isn't experienced enough to do it alone."

"Well, as a mother, I can understand that."

"Me too, Ginna." Her voice cracked suddenly, and I realized we still didn't know exactly where her children were.

"I'm sure Alexia and Andre are safe with Raina and Jael," I said, patting her arm.

She nodded and shook her head before she spoke again, changing the subject, "Still, if it really is the Lord talking to her, she should obey."

"I know. And I'm glad she obeyed when she came for Annemarie."

Suddenly my voice left me, too, as I thought of all the changes in my life since then—especially meeting Garek.

Daiah must have sensed something was disturbing me because she changed the subject again, "Boy, Ginna, I've been pulling weeds so much that when I close my eyes, I still see weeds. Why do weeds always grow faster than the vegetables?"

"I don't know, Daiah. Probably has something to do with Adam and Eve's original sin, when the Lord cursed the ground because they disobeyed him."

"I suppose that's somewhere in The Book, isn't it?"

I nodded and smiled. "It's in the very first section, called *Genesis,* which means Beginnings."

"So that's when all the problems started. Why couldn't the Lord stop them from disobeying?"

"That's always been a tough question for me," I sighed. "From what I was taught, the Lord wanted his children to have free will—to be able to choose against evil, and do good. If he'd made humans without free will, we'd just be like programmed robots, with no ability to love and have fellowship with him."

"Or with each other," she added. "So things got messed up. And it seems they still are, since we're out here hoeing weeds. Do you think it will ever be put right again?"

"There are promises in The Book about it. There's one in the book of *Romans 8:18-22:*

"I consider our present sufferings are not worth comparing with the glory that will be revealed in us. The creation waits in eager expectation for the sons of God to be revealed… in hope that the creation itself will be liberated from its bondage to decay… We know the whole creation has been groaning as in the pains of childbirth right up to the present time—"

Just as I'd gotten to this point in the quote, we heard a sudden sound above us, a combination of a buzz and a hum.

"What kind of insect is that?" I looked up and saw a bright blue belly seeming to blend into the sky above us. It looked like a dragonfly, but was much bigger than any I'd ever seen.

"It's a Drone!" gasped Daiah. "Get down into the underbrush—quick!"

I ducked and crawled beneath the closest bush. Unfortunately, it had thorns, so I didn't get as far under as I should have. The sound of the Drone suddenly changed to a high-pitched whistle, and an excruciating pain shot through my lower leg.

"AAHH!" I screamed, but then it seemed my breath left me and everything went dark.

***

"Ginna?" Daiah's voice seemed miles away. "Are you with me?"

I tried to open my eyes, but their lids felt like pieces of lead. Then her fingers began massaging my face, softly above my eyebrows and gently on my lids. Next, she rubbed my neck, shoulders, and arms briskly. Gradually, life seemed to be coming back into my limbs.

"At least it wasn't a Killer Drone." Now her voice seemed to be moving closer to me. "Can you talk yet, Ginna?"

Trying to move my lips, I found they were still unresponsive and shook my head.

By now, she was massaging my legs vigorously. Then she pulled one of my arms across her shoulders and managed to get me to a standing position. Being upright at that moment felt like a totally new sensation to my body. My feet couldn't feel the ground beneath them, and the whole forest was spinning before my eyes.

The dizziness was too much, and I abruptly lost my breakfast in a smelly pile at our feet. All I remember thinking was, 'At least I didn't vomit all over Daiah.'

"I'm sorry," my voice rasped. It was the first sound I'd been able to make.

"It's okay." I was surprised she could even hear my weak attempt at speech. "But we need to get back to the cave now."

At this point the urgency in her voice finally got

through to me. Apparently, there was danger of more Drones.

"They have heat-seekers, I think," she said quickly. "So, we won't be safe anywhere in the forest."

I really don't remember how we made it to the cave—I was probably slipping in and out of consciousness. Daiah had more strength than I realized to get me there by herself. The next thing I felt was Jon's strong arms enfolding me, and helping me down to a sleeping mat.

"Are you all right, Daiah?" came Martina's voice.

"Yeah," came a tired sigh. "Good thing it was Ginna—she's the smallest one of us."

After another fade-out into oblivion, I woke staring at the damp roof of the cave. Someone was sitting on the floor beside my mat. When a large hand reached over and took mine, I realized it was Garek.

"So now it's my turn to watch at *your* bedside," he smiled.

I felt my lips try to smile back at him, as I gradually got my eyes to focus on his face. "What happened?"

"They say fortunately it was only a Stun Drone, Ginna. The effects will wear off in a day or two. It's lucky you weren't alone out there."

Lying there looking up at him, the fuzzy confusion gradually began to clear, and I finally felt safe again.

***

It took many days, it seemed, before I could sit up and eat. This time it was Garek who was spooning soup into my mouth.

"See, I get to pay you back," he grinned.

On the far side of the fire, I could now see the others seated and talking in hushed voices. I caught a few words:

"… why I told you not to go out alone…"

"I know, Dad…"

"I've learned my lesson…" This sounded like my daughter's voice.

"…but why let them go now, when it's even more dangerous?" This louder voice with an angry tone was definitely Martina's.

"Mom, I just feel so strongly this is what the Lord wants me to do." This was Celestia's voice for sure, talking about the 'calling' Daiah told me about.

Then suddenly Jon's voice came through loud and clear, "It's apparent now that the Drone got away with a sample of Ginna's DNA."

"What are they arguing about?" I whispered.

"I'm not sure, but I think Celestia has a plan Martina doesn't approve of."

"What about Jon?"

"Let's talk later, Ginna. I can see you're tiring quickly." He pulled a blanket up to my chin, and grinned as he tucked me in. "Now, you need to get some beauty sleep."

"What? I'm not beautiful?"

"Shh! You know I think you're the best thing on two feet. Now just rest."

"Okay," I sighed, closing my eyes and snuggling down into the warm blanket.

***

The next time I woke, I was feeling much stronger and even managed to sit up while Daiah was feeding me.

"Where's Garek?"

"He and Jon are out checking the area for Patrols and Drones. And probably discussing strategies."

"What's going on?"

"Garek and Annemarie want to go to the Fountain as soon as possible, and Celestia feels she's the one who should take them."

The bottom seemed to drop out of my stomach for an instant. "But I don't want them to go without *me*!"

"Garek realizes that. He's convinced Celestia to wait until you're stronger. Besides, you're the one who needs to get away from here as quickly as possible."

"Why?"

"Because the Drone that sampled your DNA will make it possible for the System to track you—and maybe the rest of us."

"Because Martina and I were with Garek and the girls in that prison in Tornatoh, right?"

"Yeah, all five of you left DNA in there, I'd say."

"Does this mean they can connect us all, and everyone is in danger because of me?"

"I don't think Jon knows for sure. But he does think they'll be especially focused on the two of you who are from the past," Daiah added.

"They can tell that from my DNA?" My blood ran cold at this thought.

"How do Jon and Martina feel about this?"

She looked into my eyes for a moment before she answered. "Martina is very upset at the idea of Celestia taking you three alone, but I think Jon realizes it's the only reasonable plan at this point. Now, you'd better finish this meal, if you want to make this trip, too."

After a couple more days passed, I was finally strong enough to join the others around the low stone table for dinner. As we sat on the floor or small chunks of wood or stone, each of us ate in silence. No one seemed to want to start the conversation we all knew was inevitable.

Finally, Garek stood and turned to Jon. "There's no point in ignoring it any longer—we three are a burden to you. We're eating your meager food supplies and causing more dangers to seek you out. These attacks are because of our prison escape. We've drawn the enemy's attention to you."

I nodded and saw Annemarie reaching up to take her father's hand.

"Perhaps," said Jon. For a moment, he touched the old black book on the stone floor beside him. "We may never know if your presence has changed this time-line for us, or if these attacks would have come anyway. But we do know Ginna is in danger now. Still, I've come to believe the Lord has a reason for allowing you three to be here with us."

"What reason could that be?" Garek's voice sounded puzzled.

"We don't know, yet," said Martina, standing up beside him now. She reached for his hand. "I still don't know exactly what the Lord was doing back in Salien, when we were drawn to each other."

I expected to see Jon bristle at this comment and was very surprised when he didn't.

"I know I didn't behave as the Lord wanted me to, at first," she continued softly. "But I do believe he brought something good out of my mistakes." Now she was looking at both Annemarie and me.

I took her hand and pulled her down on the log next to me. Neither of us spoke, but some silent communication linked us, as though we were still together in mind and body, the way we'd been during Jon's Parallel Universe Experiment twenty-five years ago.

"Garek and I really need to cross the GAP to the Fountain," Annemarie said then.

"It's in a hazardous area," said Jon.

"And this area isn't?" asked Garek.

"Well, it used not to be," Martina sighed.

"Perhaps we need to divide up and leave more than one trail," said Garek. "That way, maybe some of us will escape."

Jon nodded. "According to the last reconnaissance report we had, Jakob and Myra are still at the outpost near the Fountain. If Celestia was to take you three…" He nodded to Garek, Annemarie, and me.

"Wait! Jon, you said you didn't want Celestia to go alone." Martina cried. "And how old is this report? Can we trust it?"

"I'll try to follow them as soon as I can, Hon." He gently took her hand in his and drew it to his lips. "But I'm needed here to get you to a safer place, and the children if we can find them. There isn't anyone else GAP-trained who can help with that. We're going to have to abandon this area altogether."

"I keep thinking of Dominic for some reason," Daiah finally spoke up.

"You know, I have been, too," Jon turned to her. "I'm wondering if his experience as a Rebel could help us."

"But we have no idea where he is," sighed Martina. "He always keeps well-hidden."

"True. We'll have to cross several times to find Dominic. It's going to be a complicated search, and I'm the only one here who can accomplish that."

I could tell by the tone of his voice this was not a boast, just a statement of fact.

"I could go with Ginna and Celestia," said Martina, "To help direct the crossing."

"I wish I could let you, Hon. But I need your power to guide *my* crossings to certain people, the way you did when you and Ginna went to Tornatoh."

"Why can't someone else do it?" she snapped.

"Because it's your blood relatives we most need to find," he said patiently.

"Like Jael?" I could tell by the change in the tone of her voice that Martina was being torn by the duties to her brother and her love for her daughter.

"And Darien," whispered Daiah.

"Perhaps your mother, too—not to mention your Uncle Dominic." Jon put his arm across her shoulders as he spoke, and she began to tremble with sobs.

"I know," she moaned. "I just wish it didn't all fall on me."

"We each have a role to play in this, Martina," I sighed. "I'm sorry to be causing you this choice. You've been apologizing to me for what happened in Salien, but now it's my turn to apologize."

Celestia moved to her mother's other side and took her hand. "Mom, I've been called to play a certain role, too. Please don't make this any harder for me than it already is. Dad has taught me well. I can cross space as well as time."

"But we're all still stuck here on this Earth!" Martina's tears were flowing freely now.

It was wrenching my heart to watch them, especially since I knew my daughter and I were the cause of this problem.

"Jael would always have some quote from The Book for a time like this," she sighed.

Thinking of Jael also brought Splash to my mind. I hoped they were safe somewhere. Picking up the ragged book Jon's feet, I opened it.

"I have one, if that will help," I said. "It's in a section called *Joshua*: 'Be strong and courageous. Do not be terrified; do not be discouraged, for the Lord your God will be with you wherever you go.'"

Again, Martina's eyes locked with mine, and this time I could feel her trying to draw some strength and comfort from me. I fervently hoped I had enough to give. Then I realized the hope both of us needed must come from the Lord.

***

Despite Martina's hesitance and anger, Jon insisted he take her and Daiah in search of Dominic. This meant the rest of us had to stay behind at the cave. And since Celestia was the only one with GAP-crossing expertise, she was in charge.

I thought they would be gone for weeks, so I was really surprised when just a few days later they reappeared. The air just outside the cave shimmered the same way it had when they disappeared. We were elated and ran to greet them. But there were looks of grief and exhaustion on all three faces.

"What happened?" I asked. "Did you find Dominic?"

Jon nodded silently, looking at the ground.

"What's wrong, Dad?" Celestia demanded.

"Nothing. It's okay. We'll need to get ready to travel, though. A lot of things have happened."

Daiah was standing silently, also staring at her feet. Then I saw she was crying, and I took her aside. She looked into my eyes as I handed her a piece of cloth to wipe her tears. "What is it?" I whispered to her. "Is Dominic dead?"

She shook her head, and I could barely hear her murmur, "Dominic is fine. It's Darien…"

"You mean, he's-"

She just nodded and sobbed even harder. I found a niche in a back section of the cave, where we could be alone.

"You can tell me whatever you want to, Daiah. I'll just listen, or cry, or anything you need."

"Thanks, Ginna. You're right. Maybe it will help if I tell the whole story. But if I start to cry too much, please be patient with me."

I put my arm around her shoulders. "Of course," I murmured.

CHAPTER 17

DAIAH'S STORY

You don't really know a lot about me, Ginna *[Daiah began]*—except that I was with the Redlarks, back when we were still on planet Terres, before you came.

["I was there 'within' Martina for awhile, though," I said.]

Well, I didn't meet you there. But it seems the Lord has seen fit to interweave me with the lives of many in this story—especially Jael and Raina. I first met Jael when Jon brought him to the Redlarks' camp near the Terres Peaks, but I think I'll wait on that part of the story. I'm not ready to tell it.

[She sighed deeply and I began to see that bringing back these memories was painful for her.]

Okay, *[she took a deep breath, as if beginning all over again].* As you know, we all eventually made it to Earth. Raina and I met because we both knew Dominic. I went to him after Jael fled the Redlarks with Jon. I admit I was feeling confused and lost. Life with the Redlarks was nearly all I knew, and I wasn't sure I could survive away from them.

But when Dominic brought me to his shelter to ask what I knew about Jon and Jael, I realized perhaps I could go with him and try to leave my old life behind. So even though I wasn't able to tell him enough for Irina and Raina to find Jael, at least I found acceptance with them—and hope for a new life.

Raina and I soon discovered we had something else in common. We'd both been raped by Amian, the Redlarks' recruiter—so we each helped the other deal with the trauma. As you know, we finally made it to Earth with help from Dominic and the Rebels. And to our surprise, Jon, Jael and Martina had also gotten there when they found Darien and the Rebels with him. By the time we all found each other, Jon and Martina were married. Raina was overjoyed when she was reunited with her dearest childhood friend, Jael.

It seemed for awhile that all would be well, but after about fifteen or twenty Earth-years passed, the System found us—and attacked Earth.

Anyway, that's all over and done. You need to hear about our most recent crossings, though it seems like another lifetime to me now. As you saw a few days ago, Jon, Martina and I stood in our GAP circle and crossed.

238

We emerged from the GAP in a totally unfamiliar place. Jon said he was using old coordinates for an isolated Rebel Out-clave. I fervently hoped someone would still be there who could help.

As my eyes began to focus again, the scene around us shimmered, and tall trees and dense undergrowth loomed around us.

"Where are we?" whispered Martina.

"Not sure yet, but it looks like a rainforest. That could be anywhere along the equator," said Jon.

"I didn't know there were any rainforests left on Earth," said Martina.

"Well, I'm not sure about that," he sighed. "But I know we're still on Earth, and this *is* a rainforest."

Soon we were trying to find our way through the dense undergrowth. It made our going very slow, and it was difficult to tell if we were moving in a proper course or just going in circles. The variety of the vegetation was amazing—every tree and shrub we came to was a different type. Some had broad dark leaves, and others had small paler ones, but the variety of shapes was overwhelming. I'd never seen a place like this in my life.

We'd just passed a very large tree with reddish bark, when Jon suddenly stopped short. Right in front of him was a man dressed all in green, and he was holding a spear—pointed directly at Jon's chest.

"We greet you in the Name," Jon whispered softly.

"In whose name?" the man frowned.

"The only name in Heaven and Earth by which we may be saved," Jon spoke again, motioning for us to keep silent.

"And that name is?"

"Kristos, the True Lord," Jon breathed.

The spear was lowered.

I let out a long sigh, and this was when I realized I'd been holding my breath. The man didn't speak again but motioned with his head for us to follow. After he'd led us a few hundred meters through the undergrowth, he turned abruptly and walked right into a hollow space at the base of one of the largest trees I'd ever seen.

Inside the tree there hung a rope ladder, and this he mounted quickly. Jon followed, and so did we. As we climbed, the insides of the tree began to close in around us. Just as I wondered if I would fit through the opening above my head, the ladder stopped. At this point, our guide scooted out through a hole in the side of the tree and pulled himself onto a sturdy branch. Once we'd joined him, he reached back and pulled the ladder up through the hole, so no one could follow us.

When we all crawled out, we saw this branch was part of a platform built around the entire girth of the tree. It expanded outward and steps led upward to a higher platform, as well.

"Wow, a house in a tree!" I mouthed to Martina. She smiled and nodded.

Soon we were seated in a semi-circle of upended log pieces. Our guide was there with two others. All of their hair was cropped very short, and I couldn't tell if they were men or women. Once a cup was passed around with some kind of herbal tea in it, they nodded to Jon, as if to say he was now allowed to speak.

"We've come from North America," he said. "System forces attacked our Safe-Zone."

"As have many we've seen," nodded one of the listeners. "Dark and evil forces are rising."

"Even worse than the System," added another.

"We're seeking Dominic's help," Jon said then.

"The one they call the Twin?"

Martina nodded.

"He's gone into hiding, and we haven't heard where," said a listener.

I felt my heart sink and heard Martina sigh.

"Has there been any word here of Darien?" Jon asked.

Now my heart began to pound, but I saw two of them shaking their heads.

"Last we heard, Darien was leading an attack to the north." I had to strain to hear this one's quiet voice.

"Do you know the coordinates?" asked Jon.

One of the listeners nodded and gave a sign with his hand.

I didn't understand what this meant, but evidently Jon did for he nodded back and gave a slight smile.

"You must stay here and rest with us tonight, before you move on," said the smallest of the three. "We have food for you, also."

"We're most grateful," said Jon.

So, we shared some type of waybread and more herbal tea with our new hosts. There were also some sweet juicy fruits with yellow skins. Inside, when they were split, was a creamy orange meat. It reminded me of a fruit called peaches that we'd sometimes had in our old camp. But there was a different taste, a bit sharper than peaches, and the fruit's meat was firmer.

After our meal, we were shown to a higher level of the tree-house where sleeping mats had been spread for us. At first, I found it uncomfortable to think of sleeping so high in the trees, but soon the soft sounds of the wind rustling the leaves around me became a sort of lullaby, and I found myself drifting off to sleep.

"Hey, Jon," I heard Martina whisper. "This reminds me of a song my mother used to sing to us when we were small."

"What song?"

"It says: 'Rock-a-bye, baby, in the tree top. When the wind blows, the cradle will rock. When the bough breaks the cradle will fall. And down will come baby, cradle and all'…"

"I'm not sure I like the sound of that," Jon chuckled. "I don't really want to fall out of this tree."

"It's just a silly children's song," she said.

"Well, I've never heard it. Thanks for singing it to me."

I could hear the smiles in their voices. Before I fully realized it, tears were filling my eyes. What I wouldn't give to see Darien just one more time. I promised myself that if I did see him again in this life, I'd ask if he remembered Irina singing that song to him.

CHAPTER 18

FROM TREE TO ROCK
(DAIAH'S STORY ENDS)

After we had some more fruit and bread for breakfast, Jon got the coordinates for Darien's last known location and gathered us into our small circle of three again. This time, as we emerged from the GAP, we were in an evergreen forest, similar to ones we'd seen in North America. This one however, was on the side of a steep mountain. Above us were bare snowfields, and below was a narrow body of water, flanked by steep walls.

"This is beautiful," I breathed. "But it looks too steep to climb."

"Well, we have no choice," sighed Martina.

Jon only nodded and motioned for us to join hands with him. In single file we moved cautiously along a narrow path, picking our way across the slope. Above us loomed steep rock walls and snow, while below were long slopes of loose rock, with evergreen trees clustered thickly at the bottom. I certainly didn't want to fall down there.

I was just beginning to feel a bit more confident, and the foot trail had widened a bit, when we came to a torrent of rushing water falling right across our path. Martina was ahead of me, and skillfully crossed on some large stones scattered across the foaming stream. But I found myself frozen in fear, hearing the loud sound of the tumbling water. This was no little rivulet—it was a full-fledged waterfall to me. Jon must have sensed my fear before I said a word, for he took my arm just above the elbow.

"Here, I'll help you across," his calm voice said.

My feet seemed glued to the path, refusing to move. Martina reached back toward me, but her outstretched hand was about two meters beyond my grasp.

"Don't be afraid, Daiah," she smiled. "It's just a little mountain stream."

"Little?" I managed to gasp.

"Put your left foot on that green rock."

"Okay, Martina, I'll try." Taking a deep breath and feeling Jon's firm grip on my arm and waist, I stepped to the green rock.

"Now put your right foot on the next one," Jon said into my ear. I could feel his hand guiding and lifting me in the right direction.

He must have placed his feet on the rock I'd just left, for he had enough leverage to help my outstretched hand reach Martina's. As soon as she had a firm grip, she pulled me toward her and held me tightly in her embrace.

Just then, there came a loud splash and a sharp cry behind me. "Ow!"

"Jon!" screamed Martina.

When I whirled around, I saw him sliding down a cascade of white water dropping about three meters. My heart jumped into my mouth, and I heard my own voice cry out, "Oh Lord, help him!"

Then somehow, he managed to get hold of a tree trunk clinging to the side of the cliff. Hanging onto this tightly, he regained his footing on some rocks. Slowly and gingerly he worked his way up, pulling hard against the crashing waterfall.

I suddenly realized I was holding my breath and mentally willing his every move. At last, he got close enough for Martina to reach down and grab his hand, pulling him into her arms.

"Oh, Jon!" she breathed. "I can't go on without you!"

"Me neither!" My voice came in a gasp.

With his other arm, he pulled me into their embrace. "Group hug," he barely whispered. "Sorry I'm so wet and cold."

"Better than dead!" sighed Martina. "Wish we could start a fire to dry off."

"No, there's too much risk of being spotted by the wrong eyes. Let's just keep moving. That'll warm me up."

Gradually we kept climbing upward, and the path widened a little more. After we'd gone what seemed like another kilometer, it took a sharp turn and doubled back on itself.

"This is what they call a switchback," Jon said breathlessly.

"Why is it so hard to breathe?" I asked.

"We're at high elevation, I think," he replied.

That had taken too much breath it seemed, for he didn't speak again until we'd made another of his switchbacks. This one led into a dense stand of prickly evergreens.

"Spruce trees," he said.

"Ouch!" Martina cried suddenly.

"What?" I asked.

"I was just trying to get a handhold, and this tree bit me!"

"Yeah," Jon smiled. "These spruces are spiky, so don't hold hands with them!"

"I get the message now," she said, rubbing her hand against her pants leg.

"Where are we anyway, Jon?" I asked.

"By the coordinates they gave us, I'd say northern Europe. I think we're near the border of taiga and tundra."

"What are those?" I was beginning to realize I didn't know much about Earth's life forms.

"The tundra is where it's too cold—or the growing season is too short—for any trees to grow," said Martina.

"It's either in high altitudes or high latitudes. The taiga is the dwarf forest at its borders, where trees can barely grow."

As we walked further up the trail, I began noticing much less variety in the vegetation here than we'd seen in the rainforest. There were only two or three kinds of trees, and they were looking smaller now and more deformed. Many of the flowering plants were the same variety and growing close to the ground.

"I need to learn more about this, if I'm going to survive here in the wilds," I sighed.

Martina smiled and nodded. "We'll help you, Daiah."

Just as she spoke, there came a whistling sound ahead of us on the trail.

"I hope that's not a Patrol," I whispered, "Or something worse." All this talk of new and strange evil forces was making me nervous.

"No, it's a Rebel signal," whispered Jon. "I hope there's another GAP-crosser with them."

"What does that mean?" I hissed to Martina.

"Maybe—if they can help us—Jon will be freed up to help Celestia and the others find The Fountain," she said.

"But we still have to find Dominic first, Hon," Jon sighed.

Before anyone could reply to him, a tall man was standing in front of us, blocking our way. He was wearing clothing with irregular patches of green and brown, which helped him blend into the rocks and vegetation around us. "Halt!" he said sharply.

Jon stepped forward and said a soft word I couldn't hear. The man nodded and motioned for us to follow.

"Guess our treetop friends gave us the correct password," Martina whispered to me, as we followed yet another Rebel guard.

This time the camp was in a bowl-shaped cove set back in a field of huge boulders. More of the low spiky spruce trees were growing in a protective ring. Because many of their windblown branches were actually growing parallel to the ground, it was impossible to see through the thick branches into the camp. And once we were in the camp, it was also difficult to see out.

As soon as we were seated at what appeared to be a dead fire ring, I immediately recognized the young man standing guard there. It was Branden, who was married to my friend Morgan. They'd been part of Darien's guard at our old Safe-Zone. He was sitting directly across from me, and when he saw me, he leaped to his feet.

"Daiah, it's so good to see you!"

We were locked in a tight embrace before either of us could say another word. At last he let go of me, and I asked the question most on my mind, "Do you know anything about where Darien is?"

He nodded but looked at the ground, not meeting my eyes.

I asked softly, "Morgan—is she –?"

He looked up and I saw tears on his cheeks, "She was killed in the most recent battle."

Now we were hugging each other again, but this time it was for grief not joy. Once we finished wiping our tears, he drew me away from the circle. "I need to take you to someone," he whispered. "Leave Jon and Martina to take care of the business."

He led me away from the cold fire ring and into a small cleft between two house-sized boulders. As we ducked down, I wondered what all this meant.

Then I saw a familiar form lying on a low pallet up against the back of a small room between the rocks. Branden let go of my hand then, and stepped back, so we could be alone.

"Darien?" I knelt beside his still form, wondering if he could hear me.

"Daiah? Is that really you?"

I took his hand, squeezed it tightly, and lifted it to my lips. "Yes, my love."

His eyelids fluttered open, and I saw a glimmer of the old spark in his eyes.

"How did you find me?"

"Jon brought us. We're looking for Dominic." I didn't want to waste time on our whole story. I could tell he was very weak.

"Are Andre and Lexi safe?" he breathed.

I tried to nod and kept gripping his hand. "I think so. They're with Jael and Raina." I didn't want to trouble him with my fears for the children. Tears were beginning to form in my eyes, dripping down my cheeks and onto his fingers.

Then he drew me down toward him and kissed my lips softly. "I'm glad you're here, Daiah. But you mustn't grieve. I'll be seeing the Lord's face soon, and there will be no tears there."

I could only nod again, for there weren't any words left in my mind.

"I love you, Daiah. No one has ever meant as much to me as you do."

"I love you, too. Please take me with you—to this place you call Heaven."

"You'll come when it's your time. And I'll be there waiting for you."

Again, all I could do was nod. Slowly he drew me closer, as well as his weak arms could muster. I didn't bother to ask where or how he'd been wounded. None of that mattered now. All I wanted was to lie there next to him, and feel his chest rise and fall—to get what warmth I could from him. Then I realized I was being selfish to keep him all to myself and sent Branden to get Martina. After all, Darien was perhaps her last surviving brother.

She stepped quietly into the room but stopped me with her hand when I moved to get up. "You can stay, Daiah." Instead, she sat down on the other side of his sleeping mat. I lay there beside my husband and listened to the soft sound of their voices. But I have no memory of their conversation, except for a few things Darien said:

"Remember, 'Tina," he whispered, "What Job says when his whole family is taken: 'The Lord gives, and he takes away, but blessed be his name'."

"I keep trying to believe with a faith like yours, Dare," she whispered.

"Wouldn't Stephen be surprised?" he murmured.

"He sure would. Please give him a hug for me—when you get there-"

"You must take care of our mother, 'Tina."

"I will, if I can find her. We've had no word of her since your Safe-Zone was attacked. Perhaps you'll see her before I do—in Heaven." Her words broke off in a sob then, and she rose.

"You don't have to go, Martina," I said.

"It's all right, Daiah. You need to be with him now." And then she was gone.

As I moved closer to him again, he whispered, "Daiah, do you remember that song we used to sing at Gathering—*'I'll see you on the other side'*...?"

I nodded slowly, "Some of it, I think."

"Could you please sing it for me?"

Tears were already in my eyes, but at this they began to cascade down my cheeks. "I'll try. It's hard to sing and cry at the same time."

He reached up a shaking hand and brushed my cheek. "I'll help you."

So I began the song, in a wavering voice:

> *I am reaching, though I cannot clearly see,*
> *Trying to touch the one I love,*
> *Thirsty for the source that's flowing from your throne…*

He was too weak to sing, but I could see him mouthing many of the words:

> *And when the story fades and disappears,*
> *And all the colors bleed to white,*
> *I'll try my best to remember all of this—*
> *Darkness broke and poured out light,*
> *Song of angels come, and send the light.*

> *When I close my eyes and shed this life,*
> *And time no longer flies,*
> *I'll find my prize hidden in the light,*
> *And I'll see you on the other side…*

Then I nestled next to him, on the narrow mat. "Here's one more song I think you know," I whispered. Stroking his dark hair, I began to sing the song Martina had sung to Jon:

"Rock-a-bye, baby…"

His lips formed a smile. "Mother used to sing me that."

"I know." I touched his lips with a fingertip. "Martina told us."

We both closed our eyes then, and I finished the song.

No one disturbed us, and I must have fallen asleep. When I woke, I could tell he was gone. His eyes were closed, and he lay totally still. There was no breathing or heartbeat, but there was a very peaceful look on his face.

"Farewell, my one true love," I whispered. "No one has ever meant as much to me as you…" These were some of the last words he'd said to me, and they were all I had left now.

I knew I should try to find someone and tell them, but I couldn't bring myself to leave him, even now. And so, I just lay there beside him and waited in the silence.

At last Branden found me and gently drew me to my feet. "There's nothing more you can do," he whispered. "We have bearers who will prepare his body. We have no place to bury our dead in these steep stony mountains, so our only choice is cremation."

"How will he have a body in Heaven?"

"The Lord will give each of us a new heavenly body, when it's time, Daiah. It says in the book of *Job:* 'Even though my body is destroyed, yet in my own flesh shall I see God, with my own eyes, and not another's'."

I tried to nod, but tears were blinding my eyes, and he had to lead me out of the small room between the boulders.

["Oh, Daiah!" I sobbed. There were no adequate words, so we just kept on hugging each other.

"It's good to be able to cry, Ginna. Not that I haven't many times already, but I think I'm finally getting to a place where I can accept that I won't see him again until Heaven.

Then she resumed her story:"]

For the next two days, Branden and I spent a lot of time with each other, talking about our loved ones. I was aching to see my children and knew he felt the same. But all we could do was hope they were safe with Raina and Jael.

The third day, Branden helped me send Darien's ashes into the wind from one of the high ridges above their camp. I really wanted to stay there, but knew Jon and Martina needed me, because I'd been close to Dominic, too.

So, in the evening of that same day, Jon took our hands, and our circle of three crossed the GAP to a place we hoped was closer to Dominic's hiding place. Martina focused all her energy on her uncle as we crossed.

This time our eyes were met by a huge body of water. It was so large we couldn't see the other side. A turbulent sea of blue stretched all the way to the far horizon.

"Where are we now?" I asked.

"If the coordinates I used were true, we're on the shores of either the Indian or the Pacific Ocean," said Jon.

"Well, I can see it's an ocean," shrugged Martina. "But what land are we on?"

"That I'm not sure," Jon admitted. "All I know is we need to look for some sea-caves along this shore. According to the Rebel leaders in Europe, Dominic may be in a place like this, but they weren't sure. He's kept his location a secret from everyone. So Martina, let's hope your power to focus has brought us close enough to find him."

***

We spent the next two days trudging along the shore—over sandy beaches, skirting rocky cliffs, and then across shorelines of paving-sized stones.

At the end of the second day, as the sun was dropping into the ocean like an orange ball, we saw a pair of caves in the cliff above us. They looked like eyes staring out to sea. There was no path, but Jon led us up toward the caves by finding small footholds in the rock and helping us climb as best he could. I tried not to be frightened, but if I happened to look down, back toward the rocky beach below us, I felt very sick and dizzy.

It was almost full dark when we finally reached the entrance of the first cave. There was a faint flashing on the walls as if a blaze was inside, and sure enough there was a small cooking fire. Beside it was a man with long white hair. He was clad in dusty brown clothes and stirring a pot warming over the flames.

"Uncle Dominic?" Martina barely whispered.

He turned toward us suddenly, in surprise. Then a smile appeared on his wrinkled face. "Is that my niece, Martina?"

She practically flew into his arms. "You're the only family I have left!" she sobbed into his shoulder.

He hugged her tightly, smoothing her hair and murmuring, "There now-"

Then he looked up at me with a question in his eyes. "Hello, Dominic," I said.

"Daiah?"

"Yes, it's me." I found I was crying again in spite of myself.

He reached out his left arm and pulled me to him, too. "I have enough arms for both my girlfriends." He let us cling to him as long as we wanted. Then at last, he said, "All right, I need to check this stew before it burns. Especially now that I have guests for supper."

When he turned to the fire though, Jon was stirring the pot for him.

"Well, I see Jon can cook, too!" he chuckled.

"That's the only reason I married him, don't you know," laughed Martina.

"Let's see if it's ready, Jon," he said then.

Jon began to ladle the soup into the bowls Dominic handed him. Then we noticed there were five bowls of soup sitting on the low rock table.

Just as we saw this, someone stepped out of the shadows, and Martina gasped, "Mother! How did you get here?"

She smiled. "There's a side passage to the other cave."

"No, I mean, we thought you were-"

"I decided I wasn't ready to die. Once we evacuated the Safe-Zone and I found Dominic, I realized I still had a reason to go on living."

As I looked more closely into Irina's eyes, I did see a light there I'd never seen before.

"And I'd learned of some healing herbs—from a friend of mine here in Indonia," Dominic added.

"So that's where we are," said Jon. "We used Martina to guide us, hoping she could locate you."

"And it worked!" Dominic chuckled. "You're on one of the many islands of the southwest Pacific, where it merges into the Indian Ocean. Come on, let's eat before the stew gets cold. It's not the tastiest stuff anyway, but it's dreadful when it's cold."

We all set to work on our bowls. Martina seemed unable to take her eyes off Irina, as though she might be a dream that would disappear.

"Mother, I have to tell you-"

"My sons are dead, aren't they?"

Martina nodded but seemed unable to speak. I saw tears glistening on her cheeks as she reached over and took her mother's hand.

"Darien died in the Europa Out-clave," said Jon at last. "We don't know where Jael and Raina and the children are."

"Then my son Donmal may be the last of the Sullien line," sighed Dominic.

"No!" I cried. "There's Andre and Jace!"

As he nodded to me, I was telling myself to keep believing that the children were safe somewhere, somehow. Why hadn't we heard anything about them by this time?

Meanwhile, Irina drew Martina into her embrace, and whispered into her long, dark hair, "The Lord gives, and he takes away."

" 'Blessed be the name of the Lord'," said Martina. "Those were some of Darien's last words. His faith became a beacon for all of us."

"Who would have thought?" Irina smiled. "When he and Stephen were young, it seemed he'd never find the

Lord. None of us could have imagined that our temperamental Darien would become the spiritual leader of our family."

"And yet he did—and helped us to find the Fountain, too."

"Ah, the Fountain," said Irina. "I assume that's where Celestia is—serving her Lord."

"That's right, Mother. Or rather, she will be soon. I hope they wait until we get back." Martina still had an edge of anger in her voice whenever the subject of Celestia came up.

By now all the stew was eaten, and Irina rose to clean the bowls. Then she sat down next to Dominic, and he put his arm around her shoulders in a natural motion. Jon and I looked at each other with the same question in our eyes, but Martina didn't seem surprised.

Dominic winked at me. "You see Daiah, Irina is a twin to my late wife, Karina."

"And you already know that Dominic is my late husband Steph's twin brother."

"So, we each decided we'd do just as well to marry the other twin now."

All of us broke into laughter then, and for a few moments, it felt so much better than tears.

Being together with Dominic and Irina seemed to rekindle some hope in me—and I was able to push aside the growing fear I'd been feeling, the fear of those unknown dark forces we kept hearing about.

And so, here I am now, back with you, Ginna. Soon it will be your turn to cross a GAP. I hope and pray you four will find what you're seeking.

"Yes, Daiah. And as soon as we get back, we can join you in Indonia."

"I sure hope so. It seemed like a much warmer and more peaceful place than here."

"Yeah, this world is cold in more ways than just temperature, Daiah. I hope this Fountain in the Desert is a warm place. I only remember glimmers from Martina's memory of it."

"And *I* hope you have safe GAP-crossings. So that we'll be together again soon, Ginna."

CODA

As dawn was bringing first light through the trees of the forest, four people stood in a circle with hands joined. Many tears had been shed and good-byes said. All of them felt numb. Celestia joined hands with Ginna and Garek, while across from her—holding both her parents' hands at the same time—was Annemarie Parker—or was it Carson?

"THE FOUNTAIN AND THE DESERT"

CHAPTER 1

QUESTIONS

The last thing I remembered was standing in the GAP (Galactic Antipaterminal Passage) circle across from Celestia, our guide. Being first-born like her, I felt the sensation of the earth disappearing beneath my feet, as though it had just fallen away.

Like other crossings I'd been on with her, I expected the ground of our destination—far across the continent—to come up and meet my soles. But it didn't. 'Something must have gone wrong.' I said to myself.

Instead, I was floating in a dense white fog, sensing nothing, not even heat or cold, for what seemed a long time. Then, bit by bit, I regained the feeling of hands holding mine. One I knew was my mother, Ginna Parker. I made out her short brown hair. Her hands had a familiar, comfortable feel, too. My other hand was being clutched by a larger, stronger hand. A man's?

Yes, now I remembered. It was Garek Carson, who Mom claimed was my long-unknown father. If this was true, my blond hair came from him, though his hair showed streaks of gray.

Gradually, the fog began to clear, and I could make out the faces of the three people in this circle with me. My feet finally felt some ground, but it was rocky and hot—not at all like the forest we'd left when we started our journey in the GAP—cutting across the dimensions of space and time. By now, my heart was thumping hard in my chest, and I pulled my hands free from those holding mine.

Ignoring the others, I stared at dark-haired Celestia. I needed answers.

THANK YOU

Thank you for joining me. If you liked the story and have a minute to spare, I would appreciate a short comment on the page or site where you bought the book.

Reviews from readers like you make a huge difference to helping new readers find stories similar to The Peaks series: *When the World Grows Cold.*

- Amazon
- Barnes & Noble
- Goodreads
- iBooks

Thank you!

M. F. Erler

ABOUT THE AUTHOR

M.F. Erler has been writing since she was about 14 years old. In fact, some of the initial ideas and characters for "The Peaks at the Edge of the World" were conceived when she was in high school, while writing assignments for freshman English class. Her lifelong goal has been to get the Peaks Trilogy out to readers, and thanks to new developments in electronic publishing, her dream has been fulfilled.

Fantasy and Science Fiction have long been among her favorite reading materials, and her favorite authors are C.S. Lewis and J.R.R. Tolkien. She is also interested in history, comparative religion, ecology, and music. Her previous publications include non-fiction articles in "Today's Christian Parent" and "Social Studies and the

Young Learner." She has worked as an Environmental Education teacher and facilitator, and also as a music teacher. Hobbies include reading, playing several musical instruments, and needlework.

She and her husband, Paul, have two adult children. All make their home in the Pacific Northwest.

Contact Frances at mferler@peaksandbeyond.com
Or follow her blog at PeaksAndBeyond.com
(MFErler.blogspot.com)